An Inner Life

(Diary of a quadraplegic)

Steve Rhodes

Contents

1

Foreword

When the idea for this story came along I found myself wondering what mileage there was in telling it. That was after I even adjusted to the notion of writing something that seemed to be a bit out of my sphere of understanding. Then it occurred to me that I had been in hospital(s) for five months a couple years back and have experienced a form of ill health that apart from some unusual behaviours was to all intents and purposes invisible. Brain diseases generally are of course...so I found myself wondering what it would be like to be visibly and profoundly unwell. I have worked with people with profound learning disabilities and as the idea germinated it became something that I simply had to try.

As I started though, the ideas came as a flood rather than a trickle. It was as if the words, and sentences were coming from someplace else. I am sure that many writers would nod and agree that the characters, if they are clear enough in your mind, and real enough in your heart, will step right in and tell the story for you. Or at the very least with you.

It was that way with this book, and many times I was struck by the connections to my own life over the last few years, what with my recovery from Autoimmune Encephalitis and such. The scene where Callum is discharged from Tooting hospital with his parents was exactly as it was for me, except that my parents are dead, so I was with my friend Lisa. I walked through the electronic doors, and paused outside for a minute to fully savour the moment. I was finally free to go home for the first time in five months, and before I knew it I was crying. As was Lisa.

We hung onto each other like a pair of frightened school kids, lost and alone somewhere deep in the woods, just as it is starting to get dark.

The next day I was writing a chapter when it struck me that the timeframe for the story also coincided with Covid 19. Just one year ago it had come strolling into every single person on the planet's life, taking away personal freedoms and pushing us all into weeks, and then months of isolation in our own homes. Many people have railed against it, and we have seen demonstrations, and some folk even flouting the law by having their gatherings anyway. We are even looking at fines now for being out in our cars if we happen to stray too far from home for no good reason.

The parallels to the central character (Callum) being *locked in*, hit me like a blast of freezing cold air. I knew that writing this would come easier, and that it would certainly add greater poignancy to such a difficult topic. After all, what were the chances of writing a book about someone who is trapped inside of his body, unable to interact with the world in a way that had previously been taken for granted? Now the whole world seems to be trapped indoors, indefinitely, and perhaps, as a result this book will connect with readers in a way that it may not have prior to the pandemic. Only time will tell if that notion (or idle musing) will hold any water. In some ways it's pretty irrelevant and immaterial to the book, but boy does it add weight and some not inconsiderable food for thought eh?

There were many parallels with my own life, that seemed to veer into my path too, and at times they took my breath away. Like the visit from Callum's friend Phil. That was taken from a conversation that I had with one of my oldest friends. He told me about his father-in-law's situation, and I just gave it a little spin, to ensure that I wasn't using the real difficulties that people encounter in their lives to bolster my writing. Having said that though, doesn't life imitate art? Or should that be the other way around?

There were certainly many days when I struggled badly with my own feelings, which have been magnified by the type of AE that I had, so the rages and bitterness that Cal experienced were often the feelings, and words of a certain writer who also at times, hates the world of humans...but deep down, his place in it. So in some ways Callum was a blessing to me, and for that I remain in his debt.

So as you read, perhaps ask yourself how you would cope with the life that the central character is now living. And when the lockdown is finally lifted, spare a thought for his life, and countless people who - through no fault of their own, just simple 'bad luck' - are in his predicament. They don't get to slip on a jacket, lace up their shoes and head out to the pub, or a restaurant to meet friends for a good meal, a beer, or a glass of chilled white wine.

Anyway, let's get on shall we? Pull up a chair and get comfortable. Oh, and if the light starts to fade, don't forget to put a light on. We don't want you damaging your eyes now do we?

'Our deepest fear is not that we are inadequate. Our deepest fear is that we are powerful beyond measure. It is our light, not our darkness that most frightens us. We ask ourselves, 'Who am I to be brilliant, gorgeous, talented, fabulous?' Actually, who are you not to be? Your playing small does not serve the world. There is nothing enlightened about shrinking so that other people won't feel insecure around you. We are all meant to shine. We were born , and that is not just some people but all of us. As we let our own light shine, we unconsciously give other people permission to do the same. As we are liberated from our own fear, our presence automatically liberates others.'

Marianne Williamsons' - A course in miracles

2

Introduction

There is a line in the film, Four weddings and a funeral, where the assembled guests at a birthday dinner party for Hugh Grant's little sister are all trying to win the last brownie, by determining who is the saddest act sitting around the table. They each take turns at *one-down-manship*, as I guess it would be called. If it had a name. One of the female characters is a wheelchair-user and argues, *'well it must be me, as I am stuck in a wheelchair, in a house full of ramps, and to add insult to serious injury I have given up smoking. My absolute favourite thing.'* I quote...almost verbatim, as I watch the film at least once a month and know most of the dialogue by heart.

What always gets me though, every single time I watch that scene is the way her husband looks at her, when she has finished talking. All of the guests go quiet when she adds that they have just found out that they can't have a baby, and her husband has such a look of utter and complete unconditional love, that I am always moved to tears. There are two main reasons why I am telling you this. You see I am confined to a wheelchair in a house filled with ramps too, and I am now permanently disabled as it turns out. I am what is popularly known as a quadraplegic. Which basically means that I cannot move any of my limbs from my neck downwards. I am utterly paralysed. Nothing moves. 'Sick irony' I call it, but irony it is just the same.

Later on in the film when Hugh Grant's character is trying to get his Hollywood actress girlfriend (played by the very lovely Julia Roberts) to stay, when she is clearly very angry, he says, *'my best friend slipped, and now she is in a wheelchair. All I'm asking for is a little perspective.'* The follow up line from her is, *'our perspectives are very different.'* That makes me angry. So very, very angry as her character dismisses him out of hand, and boy do I know what that feels like.

Odd that I am empathising with a perfectly healthy, physically able human being (well, character anyway) but I have lost count of the amount of times well-meaning people ask my mother, my father, or my sister a question about me, when actually they can perfectly well address me. I am not a fucking idiot. Quite the contrary in fact. Before the accident I worked for the National Trust as a tree surgeon, and there is a tie-in here, so stick with me. You see I was struck when I applied for the job, as on their website, there was a picture of two women chatting somewhere lush and green, with rolling hills in the background.

One of the women was holding on to a wheelchair. In the chair was someone, (like me) who had physical and what looked to be some kind of learning disability. Whilst the two women are facing each other, and laughing at some shared joke or intimacy, the guy in the chair is facing clean away from them. To me it was kind of like they had forgotten that he was human, and maybe would have benefitted from being - or at least feeling - like he was present.

Now, I get how the photographer, and all the people who chose to use the image had overlooked that little oversight, as now I am that guy in the chair, and I am screaming in rage on the inside at least. I am still a living, breathing human being. Sometimes, I wish with all of my heart that I was not. But I am.

For what it's worth.

I may be in a wheelchair every single day of my life and I am about a few shuffling steps away from complete locked-in syndrome, but for pity's sake...at least look me in the eyes why don't you? I want to scream at them, 'I am down here. Talk to me as if I am still a fucking person!' Alas I cannot, as I have not been able to talk for five years now. Not since the accident that put me in this world, that I lovingly refer to as 'The Inner World.'

So you see, all I am asking for here is a little perspective.

3

Falling

I guess that you need to know my name as we are going to get to know each other pretty well over the next few hundred pages. Well, I am Callum Ross. Pleased to meet you. At the time all this took place I was living at home with my mom, my dad and my little sister. Okay, that's enough of the niceties and introductions for now. Let me tell you my story.

I don't recall the feeling of falling. What I clearly recall in the split seconds that it took for gravity to do it's business, was something someone said to me once about falling off a horse. They said that it doesn't hurt. I recall looking at them rather oddly, as that sounded pretty random, until a split second later when they smiled and said, 'it's hitting the ground that hurts.' Boy were they right about that!

Only I didn't fall off a horse. No. In my case I fell from the top of a tree whilst trying to lop a particularly high branch. It was around February the 4th 2019. I recall the date as that is Alice Cooper's birthday, and my dad was always going on about how cool he used to be, and how he collected just about everything that Alice used to put out. Anyway, it had been a particularly cold winter and we had already seen three good falls of snow in as many weeks. For 'down South' that was fairly notable, as we often have winters where it's not uncommon to see no snow at all.

It was late afternoon. I was cold and tired, and my hands were numb from the cold. I was just finishing up, and was reaching out with the chainsaw when something snapped, and my balance all of a sudden deserted me. I glimpsed the sky and heard the remaining branches snap as I fell against them on the way down. Odd isn't it, we use the word *fall* but actually gravity is pulling us down. But I am splitting hairs there...and it makes no difference.

Christ knows how it happened as tree surgeons take tons of precautions to ensure that we are as safe as humanly possible, but my harness, or a carabiner must have failed. Maybe it wasn't set up right in the first place. Who knows? I fell over 100 feet to the ground. I mentioned in the previous chapter that I 'used to be a tree surgeon,' as since that day, I am...well, less than able shall we say?

The pain on impact was instant and huge. Briefly. That I was knocked unconscious, and didn't wake up for the best part of three months, was perhaps a blessing. Waking up at all however was the curse. Or so it turned out in the long run. Oh the irony of that last sentence.

Whilst I still care enough, I am going to tell you my story. As long as when it is done you leave me the fuck alone. Or better still do me the kind of favour that so many people who will never be in my situation judge as a sin, or an act against God, but one that for me, would end the constant grind on breathing in-and-out and from going out of my mind. Kill me!

'All know the Way, but few actually walk it.'

Bodhidharma

4

Lights

I remember seeing bright lights above me at some point, and wondering if this was the tunnel of light that people often talked about seeing when they die. But no, I think it was in the ambulance, and a medic was checking to see if my pupils reacted to light. Then maybe later it was the lights in the operating theatre. I can't be sure of anything from that time, as it is all a blur of sounds, images and dream-like confusion. Also, the drugs they constantly fed into me didn't help to keep things clear in my mind. For that though, I would likely have been quite grateful, and wish they were still pumping them into me.

I swam briefly back into consciousness in the ambulance, and I clearly recall trying to talk to one of the two ambulance crew guys who were in the back tending to me. One of them was talking to me the whole time, slowly and clearly, but in a slightly raised voice, telling me that I had been in an accident and had sustained multiple injuries. He went on to tell me that he needed to inflate one of my lungs which had collapsed, and that I also had broken my pelvis and both of my legs. I don't know why, or how I remember that time with such vivid clarity as you would think that I would have been in shock.

But I do.

I can even picture the guy, he was a huge, red-headed bear of a man, and as he spoke, he was working feverishly, cutting me out of both my harness (or what remained of it) and my favourite pair of work jeans.

I clearly recall that I asked him not to cut the jeans off as they had cost me quite a bit of money, but he completely ignored my pleas and carried on; almost as if I wasn't even there. I figured at the time that the oxygen mask must have muffled my voice, plus the not inconsiderable sound of the blaring sirens too as we careened through Surrey's busy rush hour rammed streets. A lot of that time is confused and unclear though, as everything seemed to be coming from very, very far away, and I was fading in-and-out of consciousness.

I was dimly aware that I was in no real pain, and initially that frightened me badly. I know that doesn't make any sense, but what can I tell you? You try falling over 100 feet onto a hard surface, and see how you get on with it. It just kept turning around and around in my head. How could it be that I felt no pain? Hey, I am not complaining as since the accident I get killer headaches. I guess I should call them migraines, and just being near to bright light is virtually unendurable. But why I was not in pain straight after the fall - before the world slipped away - I simply could not imagine.

I had just nose-dived out of one tall fucking tree, and hit solid concrete. I guessed that I must have been *lucky*, and as I slipped back into blissful unconsciousness, I heard one of the paramedics say, 'Christ, look at him. He's smiling for fuck's sake.'

After that I recall nothing for nearly ninety full days and nights.

5

Hospital

'I was bruised and battered, I couldn't tell what I felt. I was unrecognisable to myself. Saw my reflection in a window, didn't know my own face. Brother gonna leave me, wasting away. On the streets of Philadelphia.'

Bruce Springsteen - Streets of Philadelphia

When I *came round* in hospital, or to put it more accurately, swam *up* from what felt like the bottom of a cold, dark ocean, I tried to speak to the nurse who was standing at the side of my bed, taking my temperature. My throat felt raw and inflamed, so after trying to ask for some cold water, or juice for a few seconds, I gave up. I had to wait for quite a while until I could drink properly, without the need for all those drips that they had set up around my bed. Then, when my throat felt better I tried again, but still nobody seemed to hear me, or to understand what I was saying. After a while my desperation became so huge that I virtually gave up trying.

I know I have mentioned this before, but I was still worried that I wasn't in any pain. It must sound odd, I know. It's not that I were wishing that I was...but not to feel anything after what had taken place. How could that be? I couldn't work out if that was because of the medication, or painkillers, morphine, or whatever the hell they were filling me with. I looked down at my body which seemed misshapen beneath the thin sheets and blankets that covered it.

At first sight fear coursed through me, as my body was larger and out of proportion than it should have been, but then I worked out that it was because of all the areas that they must have put into casts. My entire torso was encased. My legs too. My arms were the only things that seemed normal, and they seemed unwilling to move. I wasn't about to try too hard to see what moved and what didn't, as it seemed a sure fire way of waking up the wall of pain that I expected to feel on return of full sensation.

I have never been in hospital for any period of time, so I spent a few minutes looking around me, and taking in the dull, beige walls and the TV screen mounted on a swing arm that could be pulled out over my bed. I tried turning my head to look at the doorway, but for some reason it wouldn't move from side-to-side. I wondered if the body cast extended to my neck, or that maybe they had put me into a neck-brace of some kind.

I did fall a fair distance and this sure looked like the end result. Well, if they had cast everything then I must be alive and kicking, and other than some pins and maybe the odd metal plate here and there, I hoped that after a few months rehab I would be as right as rain again.

Give or take.

I wondered how on earth I was going to use the bathroom as -and-when the need arose; bearing in my full body cast. I figured that whilst I was unconscious I must have been peeing through a catheter, but now that I was fully conscious was that going to continue? Maybe they would give me one of those odd looking, cardboard bottle things to use. All of these thoughts and more raced around my head as I lay there waiting to see who would come and visit.

Mom and dad came at some point in the early evening and seeing them was a shock. They had both lost weight and dad had more than just a few more grey hairs appearing at his temples. Seeing that I suddenly felt cold all over. Just how long had I been out? I tried asking them, but still my throat would not cooperate and I gave up when mom became quite distraught. She was crying when she came into the room and tried to throw her arms around me, but what with all the wires and drips that seemed to wind in-and-out of all areas, she gave up and resorted to kissing me all over my face. So, seeing me struggling to form words and failing must have been the last straw and she had to leave the room she was crying so hard. Witnessing her like that only served to send me into a fresh wave of anxiety, and I found myself struggling to breathe.

The monitor on the ventilator at the side of my bed must have triggered an alarm in the nursing station, as all of a sudden the door flew open, and in bustled a nurse and a doctor who asked my father gently but firmly to leave for a few minutes. Dad, looking horribly torn as clearly he wanted to stay and make sure that his son was okay. But he also looked afraid. I clearly remember that. He did as he was asked without question and I will never forget the look on his face as he turned and walked out. It was like he was being torn apart inside.

All that I remember once dad had left was that the doctor had red, unruly hair (like the ambulance crew guy) and a beard. He looked scruffy and not just a little tired. He spoke to me calmly the whole time, telling me what he was doing, but must have given me an injection or something as within minutes (maybe even seconds) I found myself being pulled underwater again.

Something he said to the nurse found its way into the bubble that formed around me though. 'This is the patient who has been in a coma for the last three months nurse. So please bear that in mind when handling him. If you have any questions either ask myself, or one of the other specialists.' On hearing that I recall I tried to fight my way back up to the surface. Surely there was some mistake? Then light and sound simply faded away, and I drifted down and down into blissful warmth.

But those words stayed with me.

6

Faces

Looking back now, some months later, I remember snippets of dreams, and fragments of conversations that took place around me throughout that whole time. Clearly there was nothing actually wrong with my hearing, and that had to be a good thing eh? A few times I am sure I heard my mother and father talking in low, distressed voices, but I cannot be entirely sure. It also sounded at times like my mother was crying, and dad was doing his best to comfort her. I know that he is not the most demonstrative, or emotional of men my father, but I wondered whether it occurred to him to just hold her in his arms. Words aren't always useful.

The thing was though, I couldn't see them most days, as they were off to one side of the room, or when they sat at the side of my bed, I had to turn my eyes just to make eye contact and after a while my eye muscles tired and I would stare up at the ceiling to rest them. I got to know every crack and stain on the ceiling above my hospital bed. I was still struggling to move my neck...well, my head to be more precise. I had already guessed that I had hurt my neck in the fall, and that they had put me into one of those neck-braces or some other contraption. How could I know for sure though? I still felt nothing the whole time. Well, not physically that is. More importantly though...when were they taking it off?

Again I tried to ask the doctors who came in to check my charts, the drips and the monitors how long I had been unconscious. I wanted to know the date at least, and what the extent of my injuries was...but they still didn't hear me. I had been awake now for the best part of five days. Surely my throat wasn't that badly affected?

I was screaming at anyone who came into the room. Why was nobody telling me how I was? Why were people avoiding eye-contact with me? Most of the nurses and doctors would come into my room and say, 'Hi Callum.' Then tell me their name, and chatter away happily as they did whatever task needed doing, but for the most part, that was all anyone ever said to me.

I lost count of the amount of times I tried to answer them, but for some reason, they could still not hear my voice.

Not knowing was by far the worst thing. I was trapped. Immovable and alone with my thoughts and my imagination...which ran riot. I didn't seem to be regaining much sensation or movement anywhere and there was a wild wind of fear inside me, picking up speed and intensity. Also, people still didn't seem to listen to me, or hear anything that I had to say and that didn't help with fear.

I told myself that time would heal. It's a phrase that I used to hear in eulogies at funerals. It was something that the surviving loved-ones would get told in films and TV programmes, and life imitates art. As we know. It's one of the many platitudes that people peddle in life's 'tricky' situations when they get kinda lost for the right words. I used to smile inwardly at such sayings, as clearly time won't heal the dead. I find it less funny nowadays though, and smiling is just about the last thing that I have on my mind right now.

The fear slowly coalesced and became a hot, vast desert plain of anger. The combination didn't make for a happy, or contented Callum, and my thoughts turned darker and more spiteful over time. I found myself hating certain staff members, especially some of the so-called consultants who breezed in from time-to-time to briefly talk about me, before about facing and whirling back out of the room. Didn't they ever want to ask me a question? Couldn't they answer all the questions that were whipping around inside my head constantly? It didn't seem to matter how loud I tried to make my voice, they refused to give me the time. To listen to what I had to say. That scared me badly. Perhaps my voice had been damaged in the fall too? It was quite likely and as I lay there, that realisation sank in fully for the first time. I felt cold tears track down my face, and into my ears. That I could not raise either hand to wipe them away just made it feel worse, and depression raced out of the dark corners and grabbed me with both arms.

And its strength took my breath away.

I would lay there in bed for hours on end, staring out at the grey London skyline, feeling sulky and petulant, like a small child. Underneath that though was an ever growing fear. At first it seemed to drift in starting in my stomach, like a cold winter fog. After a while though, as it really took hold, it would move upwards through my body and pull the breath out of my lungs with it's freezing, sharp-nailed fingers.

In my head, it had a face. No, that isn't quite right, it was more some kind of mask that I couldn't quite make out. The mouth seemed to be fixed in a sick looking, sharp toothed, leering grin. It looked like those terrifying masks that witch doctors wear in Africa, whilst they dance, whirling like dervishes around huge fires. Or the kind of thing you see in horror movies. The kind of thing that Jason, or Freddy Kreuger would put on. You know the type...a hockey mask I think it was. In those films the evil-doer seems unstoppable, and is hell bent on wreaking havoc. All the while going undetected by adults, or the formal justice system. They work in the dark, where our imaginations are fed by primal, deep seated beliefs. They feed off of the scent of our fear, and whilst I know this sounds dramatic, it is true to say that I now know the scent of my own fear. My imagination had all of those qualities and more.

Far more.

A few times the fear would join forces with the anger and with my anxiety too, and as a team they soon became pretty good at their respective jobs, working together seamlessly and tirelessly to infuse my imagination with terrifying worse case scenarios. I would lay there in that hospital bed, my sweat soaking the thin bed sheets, smelling my fear, terrified that my heart would simply stop beating in my chest. Or, was that wishing that it would?

Yes...at times, I wished that fiercely.

7

Voices

I am only 25 years old. Up until early this year I was playing football three or four times a week, with a local team that my dad coached. I was also a pretty good distance runner, and thought nothing of going out for hours on end, trail running up in the hills around my hometown. When not playing football, you would likely find me heading to the coast, with a mate to surf the average, and very infrequent waves around the south coast. It was something that I had tried once when on holiday with my parents in Devon, and had fallen in love with instantly. That I had been able to stand up on my very first lesson was a source of pride in me and served to fuel my passion to get good. If there was swell running anywhere around Brighton, Bracklesham or Witterings, I would get home from work, change and head straight down to the nearest surf-break.

Some days, when work was slow, my boss would take one look at me checking my mobile phone constantly for swell and say, 'for fuck's sake Callum, take the rest of the afternoon off and go catch some waves.' I loved him for that and would jump up, slap him on the back (I even tried a hug once) and literally sprint for my car, which often had my board and wetsuit in it already. *Just in case.*

I also sang in an amateur band that was doing pretty well. We had recorded a couple of demos and had sent them to some music publishers, and record labels around the UK. We were close to signing a contract with one of the three companies that we actually heard back from too, so we were really excited. I knew, deep down, that we were good. There is a sense that you get when you start hitting your stride and hear the choruses leaping out of the speakers.

I have always loved music. Ever since I was about 11 years old anyway. It all started when I was sat up early one evening, watching television. Suddenly, right there in front of me was a band called The Fields of the Nephilim. They were on some music programme or another, and they were there on stage dark, shadowy figures, enshrouded by dry ice. Their front man was striking looking, slim, long haired and dressed all in leather, with a big dusty cowboy hat pulled low over his face. He leaned away from the microphone, as the first few bars of guitar intro started and I was instantly hooked. When the whole band came in the music cut right through me, and I was aware that I was holding my breath. I let it out and shouted to dad to come and look. He stood in the kitchen doorway, with a big grin lighting up his face.

'Who's this Cal?' He asked.

'I don't know dad, but they sound and look amazing,' I cried in excitement.

He ducked back into the kitchen as the last few dying bars rang on, and I sat there feeling something ignited in me. All of a sudden I knew exactly what I wanted to do with the rest of my life. I even started to fantasise about touring, and releasing records. I would lay on my back for hours in my bedroom, just staring at the posters on my walls of all of the bands that now inspired me. I would have music blasting out all hours of the day and night, and *deep respect* to my parents that they rarely told me to turn it down.

Here is a sick irony for you though, my dad got me into Billy Idol when I was about 15 years old. He took me to see him at the Hammersmith Apollo. Just the two of us. It is one of my favourite memories. Anyways, one of the songs that stood out that night was Catch my Fall. I loved the line that followed, *'If I should stumble,'* I don't know why. I would listen to the album it was on, over-and-over again, until on occasions my CD player's amp would overheat and shut down. Then I would take it downstairs and slide it into my parent's player, if they were at work. I never got sick of that track.

If only someone had broken my fall. Or better still caught me.

Now I spend a lot of time staring at the walls, but there is no music playing in the background. There are no posters there now. They have been taken down. Thankfully. Now there is just the low, heavy hum of my thoughts and the quiet susurration of the respirator, that helps me to breath in-and-out. The sound of it makes my skin crawl, and the fury wells up inside of me, to a point where it feels like it could almost blister my skin. If anger is indeed an energy as John Lydon sang in that song *Open Up*, then mine could likely power a large city for the best part of a year.

Although, on really bad days when I am at my absolute lowest, I would have little or no desire to power anything. On those days my desire to help, or even care about any other fucker on this god-forsaken planet dries up and simply blows away. On those days, I pray to hear the respirator slowly wind down, and then eventually stop for good. On those days, I wish I were dead.

But you see, God isn't listening. Like everyone else he seems unable to hear me, or understand anything that I have to say. Or maybe, just maybe, he stopped caring.

And for that I hate his, or her fucking guts.

8

Discharge

On the 9th of May 2019, four days before my 26th birthday, I was told that I was going to be going home. It was late Friday afternoon and a female specialist (I forget her name) was making her rounds. She sat on the edge of my bed and told me that I was going to be discharged on Monday morning, and that they would provide transport around mid-day, as long as I had all of the medications and clear instructions on when to take each one. She went on talking to my parents, but all I heard was that I was finally going home. My head was whirling with those two words, 'going home.' I tried to catch her eye, but she was talking animatedly to my father and mother about all of the things they would need to have in place, and how my physio needs, after time would be something they would need to do with me, or at least to hire someone privately, and I couldn't catch her attention.

After about five minutes - in sheer desperation - I tried clearing my throat, which only resulted in my having a coughing fit. That grabbed their attention alright, but not in the way that I had intended. The specialist called for a nurse and then proceeded to bustle my parents out of the room, so that I could not hear the rest of their conversation. Meanwhile, a pretty blonde nurse with tattoos on both of her arms (Julie, I think her name was) came into the room, looking all no-nonsense, but also smiling kindly, and set about helping me to sit up, whilst the coughing fit passed.

She took my temperature for about the billionth time, then checked the one remaining drip that led into my right arm, before raising the bed sheets to check that the catheter tube was still in-place and doing its intended job. I guess it must have been, as she left with an almost full bag of very yellow, rather murky looking urine, having quickly changed it for a new one.

I called 'There's no need to take the piss' to her as she passed through the doorway, but I am not sure she heard me as she didn't turn around. Either that or it wasn't the first time that a patient had made that wise-crack.

After a while, my parents came back into my room looking happier than I had seen them look in quite a while. Mom leaned over and kissed me on the cheek, then did that thing of wiping off the lipstick marks that she had left there. So typical of a mother I guess. Certainly typical of mine. She straightened up and stood there beaming down at me with tears in the corners of her eyes. All the while dad stood at the end of my bed looking awkward and sheepish, in that way that some men do, who aren't entirely comfortable with open displays of affection.

I should explain that my dad is the epitome of a 'proper' Scottish male. With a name like Angus, how could he be otherwise? He can be taciturn, and sometimes a little too quiet, and unassuming for my liking. He was born and raised on the outskirts of a small village, on a medium sized, working farm. His parents owned the farm, and year in-year-out, made little money, but 'they always put a hot meal on the table, and gave us presents on our birthdays,' he would tell anyone who cared to listen. He would talk about them sometimes, after a few too many drinks, and I would sit there quietly listening. I enjoyed hearing about the summer harvests, and how he and his sister would go into the barns and hayloft in search of fresh eggs.

That aside, I could not have wanted more from both of my parents. Oh, my mom's name is Mary by the way. No Irish blood that I am aware of...not that the name Mary is exclusive to the Irish that is. Anyway, they were (and are) always consistent and unhesitatingly supportive in everything that I choose to do. They never missed a school play, or a single parents evening. When I decided to leave school, and rather than go to college, or university, started to pursue a career in music, all they said was they wished that they had the guts to follow their hearts, like I was doing.

After they had married, before they had kids they said that they had seriously looked into moving to the USA, but didn't quite have the heart to leave all of their parents and family, as both came from quite large, extended families. Then I came along, followed only a few years later by my little sister Melissa, and that was the end of that. No more USA.

The family settled on the outskirts of London, just over the M25 in the Surrey hills, where we led a satisfying and so far, happy life. Melissa and I were 'perfect kids' according to my parents, but I sometimes doubt that. Kids will be kids and we got ourselves into the usual scrapes from time-to-time. It's only really the same as women forgetting the agony of child-birth, and having another child to serve as a rather painful reminder that parents' memories can be selective. I don't know if that comes under the banner of 'rose tinted spectacles' as I have never understood that little idiom.

Now, here was the first truly big ripple in the seemingly happy, and I guess quite ordinary existence of just another middle class suburban family. The eldest son, who took up tree surgery to supplement his income, as he sought fame and fortune as a rock star, now lying in a hospital bed with a broken back and a catheter shoved up his penis.

'We will be in tomorrow to see you Cal,' mom was saying, 'your sister is coming in this evening with your *coming home* clothes. We bought you a new pair of jeans, like the ones that you were wearing when you had the...' her voice trailed off and she looked at dad, beseechingly.

'Before the accident.' Dad said quietly. 'Your mother and I will be back tomorrow morning son. Is there anything you want us to bring?' He spoke in that quiet, lilting accent that he had never lost, even though he had left Scotland over 30 years ago. He stopped talking abruptly, looking crestfallen, as if he had said something out of turn. I couldn't work out what the problem was, it was a reasonably innocuous question. So, why was he now standing there like he had just told me that the house had burned down?

A cold little fist closed around my heart as I saw him turn helplessly back to Mom, with big fat tears rolling down his cheeks. Mom had put one arm around his waist, whilst fishing in her coat pocket for a tissue with the other, as she was now crying softly too. I tried to say that 'No,' there was nothing that I really needed, but my voice wasn't working. I told myself it was the drugs, and that my vocal cords must be pretty much used to not making a sound, and that they just didn't hear me. Besides which I was fighting back tears myself all of a sudden.

I lay there wondering also if it wasn't just the relief of being told that I was finally coming home, and the tension and strain of my being in hospital, and mostly in a coma for the best part of three months. Or was it something more? Something that I wasn't ready to accept, or look straight in the eyes?

Not yet, for sure.

9

Home

'The journey of a thousand miles, starts with the first step.'

The Tao Te Ching - Lao Tzu

Monday morning finally rolled around following a weekend that seemed interminable. I recall sitting one Saturday night with Melissa when she was a few years younger, and watching that movie, Groundhog Day with Bill Murray, and how scene-after-scene he would wake up in the same bed, with the same radio alarm, playing the same song, and how each person he met would say exactly the same thing at the same time, in the same place. Well, the two days before I was finally wheeled into the ambulance to go home felt just like that.

I had been in Tooting hospital in a side room off a general ward for about six weeks with guys who'd had strokes, and old demented guys who would cry out in agitation thoughout the night. It was pretty depressing just laying there, watching as one-by-one they were wheeled away to another ward, or to the operating theatre, or worse still...home. They would leave clutching their plastic bags filled with clothes, pyjamas and carefully labelled bottles of medications in paper bags, saying 'goodbye' to the rest of the sad-sacks left lying in their beds, or propped in the chair at the side of their beds. I realised sadly one morning that I never knew any of their names. Not one.

Even though I was in a side room on my own, the weekend crawled by with agonising slowness. It was as if the world had all of a sudden become somehow 'denser' and everything was moving through sludge. Like those slow motion scenes they use all too often in films to give that dramatic feel to a big shoot-out or car crash. Annoyingly, there was a clock on the wall. Right above the door, that was in my line of sight, and try as I might I couldn't help but look at it. I would tell myself that I wouldn't look at it any more than three or four times a day, but then after what seemed like two or three hours I would glance up and be crushed that they hands had slowed to such a crawl, that even though I wanted it to say that two or three hours had passed, it was in fact only 25, or at the very most 30 minutes.

At times during that weekend I felt like screaming out loud. I would love to say that I could barely sit still, but you will forgive me if I avoid that kind of terminology and flippancy.

I had a visit late Sunday afternoon from my specialist, which was rare as they usually didn't come round at weekends. She did her usual thing of perching on the end of my bed, and giving me precious little eye contact. She told me that I was still going home the next day, which was a huge relief to me. Had I been able to, I think I would have lain there holding my breath until she actually uttered those particular words. *Going home.* At last I thought. She continued talking to me (at me) about ongoing therapy for my atrophied muscles, and possible speech therapy if that were called for, but I kind of drifted off and her words washed over me.

Going home. Had hearing anything ever sounded as good, or so sweet? I guess when the band started to get interest from some small, independent record companies we felt that same level of anxiety and excitement that makes it hard to sit down, let alone stay still. This news, whilst eliciting the same level of excitement in me also created a ripple of fear. It was like someone had filled a small vial with pure adrenalin, and injected it into my veins. It felt cold as it hit my bloodstream, and I was aware that I was sweating, yet felt impossibly cold.

All of these mixed emotions were boiling around inside of me. All at once. Yet unlike most people hearing that music labels had listened to, and liked their demos, or being told that you had just been given your dream job, and feeling that huge burst of overwhelming excitement that makes you want to dance on the spot, I sat there perfectly still. Utterly unmoving.

'Go figure.' As the yanks say.

I should explain. I have learned to be quiet. I have learned to accept the endless injections, the constant temperature and blood pressure checks. The changing of my catheter, and the urine filled bag that hangs at the side of my bed advertising my predicament. I endured being lifted from the bed so that the orderlies, and sometimes the nurses could change the bed sheets, or my pyjamas. In some perverse way I looked forward to the sporadic visits from the various, forgettable consultants who would breeze (often haughtily) into the room, with a cohort of young, pimply student doctors following meekly in their wake.

The pompous ass would boom some minor greeting and ask, 'and how are you feeling today?' Often getting my name wrong, and not really expecting or needing an answer. They would reel off some medical terminology that I also pretty quickly learned to tune out, and ask unintelligible questions of their nervous looking student doctors; not really expecting, or even pausing for full answers. After only a minute or so (if I were lucky) they would turn on their heels, and stride off down the ward to the hapless piece of meat laying in the next bed.

I realised suddenly that I had drifted away, lost in my reverie, and that the specialist was actually giving me full eye contact. This was so rare that I felt a little trickle of anxiety. 'Do you understand what I have just told you Callum?'

My eyes must have betrayed my fear, as I clearly recall that I didn't utter a word. She seemed concerned, as she hurried on. 'I was saying that this form of paralysis is typically the product of damage high up in the spinal cord, usually in the cervical spine between C1 and C7. The higher the injury, the more extensive the damage often is. You took a pretty good fall from what I hear. In some ways you were lucky Callum. I know that you have been told all of this, but wonder if you fully appreciate what it means for you...going forwards.'

The words 'lucky' sharpened my attention to what she was saying, and all of a sudden, I wished that Melissa (my little sister) was there so that I could hold her hand. She has a way of making me feel better, even though I was her older, big brother. The specialist went on, 'in fact, spinal cord injuries to these vertebrae are often immediately fatal because of how they disrupt control over breathing, and other critical functions. That is why we have you on a respirator and catheterised you on admission.'

At this, the specialist reached for a laptop that lay on the bed next to her. She slowly flipped up the top and the screen-saver flickered into life. It was a picture of a brown spaniel, running along a deserted beach. She blushed furiously, before hitting the space-bar. 'Sorry, that's my dog Harry, in Devon last year. I want you to have a look at these bullet points. Please make sure that you read all of them Callum. You look tired, and I am afraid that I have a habit of waffling when I am nervous. I have of course gone through all of this with you parents this afternoon, whilst you were taking a nap.'

She placed the laptop on top of the wheeled trolley that was set across my bed, and slowly turned it towards me. She pushed it closer to my face, and I read, with growing horror.

The basic symptoms of quadriplegia include:

Numbness/loss of feeling in the body, particularly in the arms and legs

Paralysis of the arms and legs (and major muscles in the torso)

Urinary retention and bowel dysfunction caused by lack of muscle control

Difficulty breathing (some quadriplegics require assisted breathing devices) and trouble sitting upright because of an inability to balance

I finished reading and I became aware that all the spit inside of my mouth had dried up. I tried to swallow but the back of my throat felt parched, like a desert. My breathing had become rapid and shallow, and I wondered for a split second if I wasn't going to vomit, or worse still black out. I lay there smelling the sour, sickly scent of my own sweat soaked body. I was filled with a sudden fury born of confusion. Why was the fuck was she telling me all of this stuff? Surely I was going home and that meant that I was on the road to recovery? Sure, the road was going to be long and as bumpy as all fuck, but I was going to recover. Wasn't I?

'I can see that you are tired and upset Callum. I will let you get some rest now. I will try to come and see you before you are discharged tomorrow.' She stood, still smiling, but this time the smile looked fake and somewhat sickly. She turned hesitantly, and left the room. 'I am not tired,' I said. But to nobody in particular. I was learning that people rarely listen to the patient lying in the bed in front of them. It's a rather odd phenomenon, but the longer you are in hospital, the more you realise that unless you need something, or make a fuss, the more the staff like it. I guess that they have plenty of other tasks, and patients to be getting on with.

I lay there terrified for hours. My mind clamoured with questions that seemed to race out of nowhere and rose to the surface like giant bubbles generated by a sinking ship. There was certainly nothing wrong with my mind as everything that she had said repeated and repeated constantly until I thought that I would go mad. All of the things that she had explained to me. Surely though she was just giving me the worst-case scenario.

Wasn't she? Or could it really be that I would lose all functioning below my neck? How would I deal with that? Could I even?

It was a long time before I finally slept, and when I did I dreamed that I was sitting in a wheelchair, my limbs twisted and shrunken. There was a bright red scarf tied tightly around my mouth. It was as if I had been kidnapped and was being kept from speaking, or crying out for help. Then the scene shifted and I was all alone, high up somewhere at the edge of a cliff. Above me the sky was filled with dark, swirling black clouds of birds. Thousands and thousands of them wheeled and spun about in huge circles in the sky, creating ripples and shapes as they grew in numbers, before finally turning as a single unit and flying off into the distance.

The oddest thing though...was the total absence of any sound.

10

The Inner World

For a while after I got home I struggled with the realities of my new life. I will talk a little more about that later though, as what strikes me about those first few weeks, and maybe even months was the 'unreality' of it all. Nothing felt like I had expected it would. There was me thinking that getting home, and back to some kind of normality would lift my spirits. Then the real healing could begin. Where did I hear that phrase though - *reality bites.*

In the first week I just lay in my bed downstairs, as now that the stairs presented issues, it had been decided that I should have what was dad's office space. My parents had gone to great lengths to get it all set up just like my bedroom with my old bed and desk, and all of my CD's were racked into shelving on the wall, above my laptop and Playstation. Even some of my old posters had magically migrated onto the walls too, replacing dad's sales charts, and the family snapshots of holidays and happier times. They had looked out some pictures taken of me singing onstage at various gigs, and placed them lovingly in one of those big, multiple shot photo holders that they sell in IKEA too. On seeing that I had initially cried. I couldn't help it.

My amplifier and two guitars had also been brought downstairs and they sat in the far corner of the room, taunting me. Not that I was ever going to be the best guitarist in the world, but I enjoyed playing, and always did my songwriting on a battered old acoustic that I had found in one of the guitar stores in Denmark Street. It lay at the back of the store I recall, a little dusty and sorry looking, but when I picked it up and strummed a few open chords, I instantly fell in love with it. The guy seemed happy when I offered to pay cash and the faded price tag of £150 dropped to £130, with the case thrown in for good measure. He even gave me a set of Fender, bronze strings for free. I left that store with a big, shit-eating grin on my face, and spent the remaining £20 in a local pub with the bassist Jez, and our drummer, Trystan.

So, there I was. Home. I should have felt happy I guess. But I didn't. The first surprise was that on leaving the hospital, with mom on one side, dad on the other and little sister pushing me in a wheelchair I suddenly fell apart. We rolled through the sliding doors and I saw the sky, clouds and trees and simply started crying. I hadn't expected it, but all of a sudden I was hit by a massive sense of loss, grief...call it whatever you want, and huge tears streamed down my cheeks. I was dimly aware of the chill in the air making them feel cold against my skin. But do you know what made it a million times worse? I could not wipe them away. And that was the second huge reality check for me. The first was being told by the specialist that I may have lasting, or permanent quadriplegia and now this cute little trick; just leaving the hospital, not even to the front gate of my own home, and I cannot lift a finger to help myself.

I could feel one thing though. I didn't need my hands, or my fingers to explore the cold, hard reality of the truth. I was now likely to be in a wheelchair for the rest of my life. It hit me with a force so powerful that had it been solid it would have killed me outright. I found myself wishing that I were dead...for the very first time.

But most certainly not the last.

So, you must be wondering how I fill my days. Well, I get up early and get dressed, have breakfast and lace up my old running shoes. Then, I let myself out of the back door, which gives out onto some fields next to a river. I follow the path that cuts alongside the river then up and into the hills around the side of Box Hill. Look it up if you don't know it. It's quite a famous view-point and on a good day you can see the South Downs in the hazy distance.

I never bother with Apps, or maps, or marked pathways and I try to never follow the same route. Having done this for some years now, that is quite hard, but I try to seek out new routes and whenever I spot a footpath, or animal trail leading across, or through some woods, I log it away in the back of my brain, and take it the next time I am out.

Today, I am running out in a northerly direction, as if I was going to run all the way into London, which you can in fact see, in the distance from quite a few points around Surrey. I have no real route in mind early on in most runs that I do. Mostly it is just whether I fancy hills, or being in woods, or forests. Sometimes I go for an easier option and take a flat route through some of the lowlands around here. It all depends on how I feel, and since the accident, it is a joy just to be able to escape the confines of my wheelchair.

As I run, I send my consciousness around my body, feeling each of the muscles in turn, and looking for tension, or niggling pains, or areas where the muscles are tight. Sometimes I bring my awareness to my breathing, and when after two or three hours my breathing is still good, and my lungs feel strong, I get that sense of elation mixed with gratitude that I am able to do this. So many people cannot, pr don't want to, and I count my blessings almost every single day. Sure, being a distance runner requires discipline I guess, but for me, it is more about the need, or overwhelming desire to simply be outside and moving.

It is when I don't or cannot run, that I feel low, moody and somehow *lost* like something precious is missing. I could theorise that it is having the sun on my skin, giving me the vitamin D that they say is vital to humans. The connection to nature. It could be that I guess as seeing animals in their natural environment, rather than on leashes, or in cages is infinitely preferable to me. It could be all of those things on different days.

Who knows? Do I even need to understand it?

Then, all of a sudden I fall. No, I haven't tripped and gone sprawling to the ground, distracted as I so often am, looking around me as I run. This time the fall is longer and harder. It is the fall that I took from the tree. I hit the ground so hard that I wake up, and find myself lying in my bed in the converted office that is now my prison cell. I am laying on a pressure mattress, which has recently become another happy reminder that with my body wasting away. As due the fact that as I am not moving I'm susceptible to pressure sores, which can then become infected. Yep, it's all fun here in 'Callum-world.'

Oh, and did I mention that my bladder and bowels no longer function as they used to? Yeah, this is a really good joke. Take a seat, though it shouldn't take long to tell it. I just hope I get the ending right. Stop me if you have heard it before. It seems that I am not doubly incontinent, as I first feared. Sure, I still need to be catheterised and pee into a bag, just like in hospital...and that might be for life! But also, for extra chuckles there's the issue of needing to crap, but not being able to. In the past whenever I needed to take a shit I simply took myself to the loo, did my business, wiped my own arse, flushed and left.

Now it seems that I cannot. Now, I suffer from constipation, which is as much to do with my not moving about so much; my almost perfect inertia. The details of quite how this gets dealt with by my mom, or my dad, I don't feel like telling right now. Maybe later, though eh? Right now, I don't feel like telling any more jokes.

Right now I feel like crying, but am scared that if I do, that I might not be able to stop.

11

Birthdays

It is my 26th birthday today. I wake up and open my eyes. The world is still there, and for a split second I wonder if the accident hadn't all been a part of some elaborate, and very vivid but disturbing nightmare. Then in the darkness, I hear the sound of my breathing. It is not the gentle susurration that it used to be. Instead it is the horrible, machine-like rasp of the oxygen mask that sometimes I wear at night, and I realise that the real nightmare is reality.

Hot tears burn their way down my cheeks and I lay there screaming inside. The reality is sinking in now. I have only been at home a mere handful of days, but already I hate my room, the bed that I spend most of my days in currently, and the pile of medications that are stacked in the corner of the room. They lay on top of boxes of incontinence pads, which I now wear at night in case I '*have an accident*.' My breath catches in my throat as a sob rises, as suddenly I recall what my sister reminded me of the other day, quite unwittingly. She was talking about my birthday, and coming home, as naturally she was excited and pleased for me. Then a look came across her face of pure panic as she asked me what I wanted. I looked back at her, and could see that she knew instantly her mistake. You see my parents had bought me a brand new mountain bike. It was a Specialized RockHopper with full suspension. They had argued that as I had been working hard, and saving every penny of my money in order that I had enough money to tide me over whilst the band were waiting for the record deal, or publishing contract that would mean having at least some income from music that they wanted to get me something special as a reward.

I had been cycling seven miles to work and home every evening throughout the winter, on an old worn out bike that my friend Stevie had sold me for £100. It was okay, but about 10 years old and was hard work when hills presented themselves. I had seen the Specialized in a local cycle shop and as it was the end of year, coming into the new year, the 2018 model was slashed to just under £1,500. I had gone in with dad one Saturday afternoon when we were coming home from a walk through the local woods.

I had raved about it when I saw it in the window, and we strolled into the shop trying to look casual. I knew the guys in the shop as they went to one of the pubs in town. Two of them played in a band that we had supported a few years back, and as I spoke to one of them about our possible recording deal, dad looked the bike over. He was good with his hands. One of those people who seem to have a knack for anything with moving parts, and I trusted his judgement and opinions whenever I bought anything mechanical, plus I am pretty impulsive and would have rushed in panting enthusiastically, like a red setter chasing a ball had I been alone.

I was still talking with Andy, but now about bikes when dad ambled over and interrupted. He asked if the bike had been purely used as a demo model. Andy said that *yes, it had.* Dad frowned at that and turned slightly to look back at the bike he said, 'really? I ask as it has some scratches on the bodywork and one of the pedals has scuff marks that make it look like it has been dropped once, or twice.' He turned back to Andy with raised eyebrows. Andy blushed furiously and said, 'oh, sometimes the staff take them home and try them out too.'

'Hmm,' dad said. 'Well then, if I offered you slightly less than the price tag states right now, you would likely take it. Wouldn't you Andy?'

Andy said that if we could wait a few minutes he would speak to the boss. We strolled over to the bike as he turned and went out to the back of the shop. 'Why are you interested dad?' I asked, somewhat foolishly perplexed.

'It's for you son.' He said, smiling slightly at me. 'It would be for your birthday which I know isn't until May, but a good Scotsman knows a bargain when he sees one Plus I hate seeing you coming home looking like a drowned rat, all red faced, having cycled that terrible old bike of Stevie's. I figure if I am going to have a famous, wealthy pop-star for a son, this will be an investment in the future.' At that he put an arm over my shoulder (a gesture that was oddly uncharacteristic for him) and said, 'I'm proud of you son. When you set your mind to do something, you sure don't do it by halves. Yer ma and I have talked it over, and she said you had been harping on about a new bike for ages now. Well, there you go,' he said pointing at the bike.

A lump rose in my throat at that and I had to look away, and fight back tears that were suddenly all too close...especially as Andy was coming back with a big grin on his face.

'The boss says okay. He also says you drive a hard bargain Mr Ross.'

My dad nodded once, and smiled at that, then slapped me on the back, whilst fishing with his other hand in his jacket pocket for his wallet.

12

Friends

Did you ever look at the word friend-ship and wonder about the phrase, 'like passing ships in the night?' I never have before, but over the last year or so the thought has occurred to me a few times. I find it odd that it has the word *'ship'* on the end of it. It suggests some kind of journey, but then when you think about it we travel through life with certain people, who we feel an affinity with, and with whom we love. I looked it up online and whilst there was much written about the word friend, the ship element was never mentioned. Not once.

We sure talk about life as a journey, and if we stick with the sea-going analogy, I would sure want the right people around me when the weather truly whips itself into a frenzy, and is throwing the ship from side-to-side so violently that just staying upright is a challenge. Yeah, the right crew members are like gold...and there again is another word that gets used for groups of friends, or like-minded folk, '*crew.*' We talk about our crew in all walks of life, including flying. Huh...weird eh? Forgive me for not rushing to my laptop and googling the meaning and derivation of the word crew though as I am currently sitting in the lounge of the house and my laptop is back in my room.

Friendship is something that I have always valued highly, and there is nothing that I wouldn't do for the people who I call true friends. Also, I guess that I am lucky in that I have a lot of them. Not hundreds you understand, and not the type that so many people my age claim to have on Facebook. The notion that anyone has over 270 or so 'friends' drives me crazy. I would call the best part of three quarters of the people, who say 'hi', or send *'friend requests'* are not the kind of people that would turn up when you most need them.

Quite the opposite is likely true, they will cast around on one mobile device or another, waiting for just the right social function to attend, then go to it. But then they spend half the night staring at their mobile phone, wishing they had gone to one of the other, oh-so attractive looking parties. That whole clingy need to have vast sums of friends, rather than ones that you are close to and care about, has always kind of irritated me. It smacks of being rather desperate, a little too insecure, and not just a little pathetic.

It seems sad somehow that just because someone 'likes' a comment on your page, then all of a sudden they are added to an ever growing list. And before you know it you magically have 300 of them all under the heading *Friends*. How many of them would come to your wedding, visit you in hospital, or come to your funeral I wonder? How many of those so-called friends would pick you up at 2 a.m. in the morning, if your car broke down in some dark, deserted lane in the middle of nowhere?

The true test of friendship however, comes when you go into hospital and spend the best part of three months there. Many of my true friends drove to wherever I was at least 2-3 times a week, depending on where the hospital was in relation to where they lived, or worked. An even greater test of friendship is putting up with hour long (sometimes longer) visits, where I have little to say, and sit there staring into space, only half listening to them talking about their jobs, or their new girlfriend/boyfriend, or telling me what they did at the weekend. *Yeah, that is a true test I would say.*

Further down the line however, I find myself wondering how many of them will stay in my life. Then my mind turns grey, and the shadows grow just that little longer and colder. I turn to the wall inside my head and throw a small ball against it. It makes an empty 'thwok' sound as I bounce it off the floor, up against the wall and back into my hands, just like Rocky did in those films Sylvester Stallone made in the eighties. This all takes place in my head you understand, as there is a complex interplay of muscles, neurons, and thoughts that go into controlling the body. All of which we take for granted when the system is up-and-running just fine. Mine is on holiday though, and I stare out of the window praying for it to come home.

Hmm, I kinda lost my way on that one. I guess what I am trying to say is that I fear that it must be only a matter of time before my friends start to fall out of love with the new me. Rather like a new car that has that sweet, new smell inside, and you are out there every weekend cleaning and waxing it. Let's imagine (as I have become quite the expert at doing) that just like that car, when it is running well and the engine purrs smoothly under the bonnet, and it takes us from A to B with never a complaint, we love it. Naturally. It's the best goddamn car we ever had. The apple of our eye.

However, farther down the line, when it starts to cough and splutter on starting, or when it gives that little hitch as you pull away from the traffic lights on the way home from a late night rehearsal and it's raining hard you find yourself chanting out louds, words of comfort and encouragement, and praying that it just gets you home. Well, when we get to that point in our relationship...we ain't talking about love; to quote Van Halen.

That's about two stops out from the station where we start calling it a 'miserable piece of shit,' slam our hands on the steering wheel in sheer frustration, and start thinking about selling it.

All of a sudden, the car we loved so much becomes the object of our frustration and dislike. I guess you may be asking where I am going with all this, as didn't we start by talking about friends, and whether the good ones stick with us through thick and thin? Yeah we did. Sorry. I have a lot of time on my hands nowadays and my mind seems to have gotten good at taking different paths and forks in the road. It keeps it (and me) entertained. And that is no mean feat.

With so much available time however, comes a lot of reflection, and recently I have started to see the synchronicity in everything. The metaphor about the new car and the old one, seems all of a sudden quite relevant. I mean think about it. I am just 26 years old, and my bodywork is no longer quite so shiny. The wheels are rusted and the brake pads too. Nothing works. It sits outside the house, or in the garage under an old faded cover gathering dust. It starts to slowly fade out of sight, as we stack boxes on it, and around it. Then, six months down the line, it is just another thing that we meant to get rid of, or sell. We tell ourselves that we will get around to it next year, or in the spring when the weather is better. After all, who wants an old piece of junk like that? I mean really?

I guess the parallel is kind of dramatic, but when you are locked inside a body that will not move, with only your thoughts for company every single day of your life, well then you kinda get that way. It's not like I am going to find a hobby anytime soon.

So, over the last six months or so, have I seen a decline in the visits from my friends? Yes. I have, if I am honest. When it became clear that not only was I never going to move again, and that just getting me to the local pub was like running a marathon, strewn with obstacles, then the daily visits slowed to a trickle, then became weekly. When it became clear to not only myself, but to anyone who knew me, that I was not actually able to communicate verbally, then those weekly visits slid slowly into monthly, and then in some cases six monthly.

In some ways I understand that. But if you asked if it affected me, or how I felt about it, then you would need a few hours to sit and listen (had I a voice) as it would take me a long long time to answer you.

Without crying that is.

13

Girlfriends

This is one chapter that I didn't want to think about, or really talk about anymore. Not since the accident. So if you have been wondering if I have, or at least had a girlfriend, then the answer is 'kinda.' Her name is Elspeth Taylor. Yeah, I know, that should be Elizabeth (then again you have that rather famous actress with the same name) but that's the name on her birth certificate. And full marks to her parents for preferring that spelling and going with it. There sure as hell is nothing wrong with being different, and if different is your thing, then Elspeth is your kind of girl. She sure is mine. As soon as we met, at a party after one of our gigs, I knew that we had to be together.

I happened to wander out onto the balcony of the flat where the party was being held, and she was there talking with some people that I didn't know. I stayed out there longer than I needed to, just to keep her in my view, and hoping that I had registered in hers. She was talking about music, so I managed to tack myself onto the little group, and dropped in the odd comment here and there. She looked at me, when I mentioned that I was the singer in a band, and that we had played tonight, in Kilburn. 'I thought you looked familiar.' That was all she said, so I asked her what she meant. She told me she was a friend of Gail's, (the party's host) and that she had seen one of our posters on a wall. Annoyingly she then excused herself, and went inside.

I played it as cool as I was able and waited for all of 2 minutes before casually strolling back inside too. She was nowhere to be seen, and my heart picked up just a little. Christ! Had she left? I went into the kitchen to look for Phil (and her) and asked him where the loo was. 'It's in the hallway, same as most flats of this type Cal, and the door that you passed on the way in.' I told him he was a wise-ass, and walked out and strolled towards the small queue forming.

'Hello again,' a soft voice said from behind me. I smiled at the sound and turned to find Elspeth standing behind me, smiling too.

'Hello you,' I said. Once again, just seeing her set my heart beating just that little bit quicker, but I tried to act casually happy to see her. If such a state exists that is. We stood there talking for a few minutes, and it felt so natural, that I soon relaxed and we found out that we had very similar tastes, not only in music but in clothing too. She was dressed head-to-toe in black, as was I. She had black eye make-up and black painted nails too. As did I, although a little subtler than hers. All a part of the image that I wanted the band to project I told her. When it came to be my turn to use the loo, I offered that she go first. She smiled and said, 'thanks Cal,' and brushed past me just a little closer than new acquaintances generally would.

Now I am not the most sensitive guy in the world, or always that aware when females fancy me, but here it was clear that the attraction was mutual. I waited for a few minutes, my mouth just a little dry, and when she came out I said, 'do you fancy going out sometime?' She looked me over, but said nothing. So I said, 'look, can I have your phone number? I would really like to see you again.'

A minute passed, then she said, 'no, I am not going to give you my number. I am fed up with guys taking my number and not calling. If you want to see me again, then come home with me tonight.'

'Okay,' I said. 'Sure, that would be great. I can give you a lift if you like, as I have a car with all my stuff in it nearby.'

'Well, good enough then,' she replied.

And that was that really. From then on we were pretty much inseparable. She lived and worked in London, so I would drive in two or three times a week, or stay over after gigs. She would come stay with me on the weekends, if that is, we weren't clubbing or going to see bands in town. Which is generally what we did. It was great not only meeting someone with a passion for music that matched mine, but who also had a real zest for life and new experiences. There was something very free-spirited about her that just felt right to me, and when I was with her I felt *complete*, in a way that I had never really experienced before.

Mom and dad both loved her as soon as they met her, and I would watch them as they talked, and laughed at the dinner table sometimes when she stayed over and ate with us all. Of course Sis loved her too, and I think developed a bit of a 'girl-crush,' as I noted that her taste in clothes moved slightly towards black, and she dyed her hair black a couple of months in too. I am sure I read someplace that *'Imitation is the sincerest form of flattery that mediocrity can pay to greatness.'* It made me smile inwardly when

I saw the way she looked at Elspeth and would hang on her every word. I wondered if Elspeth ever noticed but oddly never asked her. Oh, I am sure not implying that my sister is mediocre by the way, I am just saying that Elspeth had a way of drawing good people into her world. She kind of inspired you to be a better person. I know that may sound odd. Maybe even a little cheesy. You would have to meet her to truly get it.

The reason though that I said 'kinda' when I mentioned her being my girlfriend is that we have been on and off as a couple for about three years. We started dating when I was 22 and she was about 21 years old if my memory serves me correctly. And to say that she is old and wise beyond her years is quite frankly a huge understatement. On the flipside though, is a wonderful ability to also be wonderfully child-like in her sense of wonder. I flatter myself when I say that you have to be something special yourself to keep up with her.

I guess that in some ways we are *'best friends'* more than boyfriend/girlfriend in title at least...but Elspeth hates titles and labels, or being put into manageable little reference boxes. And I for one agree entirely with her. So we fit outside of the box, and that seems to suit both of us just fine.

Since the accident, there have been changes to our relationship though. I could be flippant and say that the physical side of things isn't quite as good as it used to be...but I am not sure that I am resilient, or callous enough to throw myself into the cold waters of such a joke. No, there is a time for going into the water and the freezing depths of winter are certainly not that time. Oh, I use the term *winter* in reference to my day-to-day mood. There is ice over the lake now and the trees are still with harsh, white frost.

Being around me now can be a bit like that. At other times it can be like sitting too close to a blast furnace, where the door is left open, and at times the heat that radiates from my bitter fury is so intense that people don't stay too long.

Where all of this leaves my relationship with Elspeth, I cannot say. We dare not look each other fully in the eyes anymore. And the truth is always in the eyes.

Always.

14

Snow

It is coming up for Christmas and my parents are trying so hard to remain upbeat, and positive around me as it is my first Christmas since the accident. I know that they are trying really hard to bolster my spirits, but everything serves as a reminder of what I have lost. My first birthday since the accident. My first halloween. My first firework night. Every first just reminds me of who, or what I am now.

So let's not beat around the bush then. Come on, say it with me. This is my very first Christmas as a locked-in quadraplegic. There now, doesn't that feel better? We all know where we stand now don't we? Well, all that is except me. No standing up here. *Not that I am bitter or anything.*

Melissa has even gone to the trouble of planting a fir tree just outside my bedroom window, and dressed it with coloured lights and tinsel. But I cannot feel it. I cannot feel how I used to about this time of year. I had always loved this time of year, and entered fully into buying presents, and silly stocking fillers for friends and family. I loved being a big brother, and creeping into Melissa's room when she was a kid to hang a stocking filled with dumb-ass presents, and small things wrapped in brightly coloured paper. Half of the idea of a stocking is to keep little kids quiet when they wake out of sheer excitement at 3-4 in the morning, and to stop them from waking mom and dad up...but who cares? I loved all of it.

We have entered into another winter, and like last year it is a particularly cold one. It is the winter of my discontent. That is for sure. Ask me if I am content to lie on my bed, or to be propped up in a wheelchair with a silly party hat jammed down on my head, and I will likely turn away from you and stare at the wall. Figuratively speaking that is.

Cars move by outside slower than usual due to ice on the roads, their headlights cutting through the early afternoon darkness, and the pedestrians who pass by my window have that awkward, deliberate gait that people adopt when they are just waiting for a foot, to slip or slide away from them.

Chance would be a fine thing, I think bitterly.

It is late at night now, and I am laying in my bed. I can see that there is snowing falling outside, and that should please me. I have always loved the snow. Tonight though my nerves feel raw and I feel as if I could match every falling snowflake with freezing cold tears, torn apart inside with a mixture of grief, anger, confusion, helplessness and a depression that seems endless, bottomless and visceral. I feel utterly and completely bleak. If I could move just one limb, I would grab for the nearest sharp object and slit my own fucking throat.

I swear to God that is all that I want right now. A final end to this waking nightmare.

I am living the sickest, shittiest excuse for a life, that at times seems like the worst joke ever told. That I am both the subject of the joke, and its punchline fuels the fury inside me. My head aches with the intensity of it, and my body itches and sweats simultaneously. The desire to wreck my room is huge. I wish that I could smash everything in it. I picture myself tearing down the posters, and hurling the guitars at the windows. I can hear the sound of breaking glass, high and perfect in my head. I imagine the blood pumping in my veins, and can almost see the neurons firing, sending signals to my muscles. And each one follows its given cue, relaying thought into action. I can almost feel the sting of pain underneath my fingernails as I rake the posters off my wall. I would relish the feel of warm blood as it seeped from tiny paper cuts. I would relish every single one.

That I cannot do any of these things fuels the fires of that rage inside of me. I can hear the blood in my veins and my breathing is loud in my ears. But I cannot feel it. I want so badly to feel something physical, and not emotional. I struggle to breathe in-and-out, as I am screaming at the top of my lungs.

Yet nobody can hear me. Not a single living soul.

15

Sleep

So here we are again. At that point where we get to shuck off the past year and slip into the new one. 2020 stretches out in front of us fresh and untrodden. Like a new fall of snow. No footprints, just blinding white silence. I for one will not be leaping around in enthusiasm, waving my arms drunkenly, and kissing all the females in the room. In some ways leaving the past year behind is a relief, but every day feels like starting at the bottom of Everest, and climbing laboriously towards the summit. And for me, just breathing in and out again is an effort.

At about 11:30 pm I realise that I need to take a crap. Which nowadays is rare, what with the ongoing battle with constipation as one of the many little gifts that my situation brings. I try to draw attention to my need by blinking rapidly, but with all the fuss about the coming of midnight, it is virtually impossible. My frustration mounts and I wish for the millionth time that I had landed on my fucking head, and been killed outright.

The minutes crawl by and my discomfort grows. At around two minutes to midnight, I can no longer hold on and end up having a bowel motion in my underwear. What a way to celebrate the passing of the old year. The shame feels total and all-consuming. It is not the first time this has happened, but that doesn't make it alright. I am 26 years old for fuck's sake, and most of the time I wear nappies to mitigate for just such an eventuality. I also cannot wipe my own arse, or even change my own clothes. The humiliation and rage grows inside of me, and I wish that I could simply fade away.

It doesn't take long for my folks to realise that the smell emanating from me isn't just gas, and they both put down their drinks, and set about hoisting me, cleaning me up and putting me into clean pyjamas. They then ask me if I want to go to bed and I wonder if the truth is they want me to go to bed, so that they can at least pretend for a while that life can go on as normal for just a few hours.

I blink once, which we have agreed is 'yes' in our limited communication, and they lower me into my bed, wish me 'happy new year' and turn out the lights.

I lay there in the dark, seething with the sheer indignity of it all. Not just the being cleaned up, and dressed by my mother and father in my mid-twenties, but at all of the stupid small things that being a quadraplegic has brought into my life. For one thing, who the fuck wears pyjamas at my age? I sure never have. Not since I was a kid anyway, and there is the rub...being like this seems to result in people talking to me, and treating me like I am retarded, or child-like at least. I am not a fucking child, I am a grown man trapped inside a useless body that has chosen to give up responding following a fall.

I want to turn over onto my side and put my hands over my face, to block out the world, but I cannot even do that. I never used to sleep on my back, and I hate that it is still a huge struggle for me to get to sleep every single night this way. Even now that I have had the best part of the year to get used to it. Such little things that people take for granted now trouble me hugely in this still, silent and unmoving world of mine. It is hours before I finally fall asleep and I wonder what all my friends are doing as I lay there alone in bed.

16

Silence

'When shall we live, if not now?'

M. F. K. Fisher - American writer

Who could ever imagine that the whole world would become *'locked in'* for over a year? Not I, that is for sure, but locked in we all are. Oh the irony of those words. Everyone around me is talking about Covid 19 and their fear of infection, and potential hospitalisation. They talk of the resultant fatigue, the muscle pain, the loss of all motivation and in extreme cases the need for physio to learn to walk, that are all potential side effects. As and when people come to visit me, they now come wearing a mask, and mom gets them to put on latex gloves too, as I am pretty vulnerable and open to any kind of infection.

Frankly, I would relish the opportunity to contract some hideous type of flu. I would welcome anything that likely would result in my dying. As long as it is relatively quick that is. If only people knew just how often I pray for such a thing, but let's not get off track here. There is a sick fascination in watching the news, and hearing about all the levels of lockdown being imposed. I listened in wonder as the prime minister announced the first lockdown and marvelled at how quickly people became stir crazy. Within just the first few days and weeks friends were saying that they hated being at home all of the time, and didn't know how they would, or even could cope.

There were stories of 'lockdown divorce,' and loads of couples splitting up having had to spend too much time in close proximity to the person, or persons that they had previously loved, and thought they would be with forever. I smile inwardly (a rare thing) as it reminds me of that line in Let's Go Crazy, by Prince, *'forever is a mighty long time, and I'm here to tell you, there's something else.'*

Who would have thought that a form of flu could be the one thing that unites the world? Oh, I am not saying it is a good thing, but a part of me cannot see that it is a bad thing either. After all, society was kind of getting lost anyway. You see people on the streets staring at their mobile phones, lost in some inner space, oblivious of the world around them. They get home and click on another screen, be it the TV or a laptop, and spend the next few hours staring at that. And you can be pretty sure that their job also entails the almost use of some kind of PC...or laptop. So ditto at work eh?

We seem to move through life now going from screen-to-screen. It is almost as if we are living vicariously through feeds, screensavers, snippets of pointless news, and stories about forgettable, third rate so-called celebrities. We have 'reality tv' which is so devoid of any kind of 'normal' that I cannot be in the same room with it. All the time we are getting distracted by unwanted ads constantly appearing in front of every news story. Adverts for sandals, hair products, dumb gadgets, pet products and shiny looking new cars. That frankly all look the fucking same!

I got sick of seeing all that shit before the accident. You can be pretty goddamn sure that I am heartily sick of it now. I cannot get up and walk away, or switch the channel over, or even ask anyone to please turn it off. Believe me, when you leave the room and the radio, television, or whatever it is that has been on in the background is left on for me to 'enjoy,' that you are in fact, often leaving me to suffer the slow water-torture that is pure inanity.

I hate listening to stupid DJ's with their all too cheerful voices, and anyone who knows me well should get that I don't enjoy mainstream music. I never have for crying out loud. How on earth being in an accident would have somehow magically changed my taste in music I cannot imagine. Unless that is, it has lowered my IQ exponentially. I have lost count of the times when people have said, 'do you want this turned up?' I sit there blinking madly saying, 'no, no, no.' They mistakenly think I mean 'yes please', turn the volume up and leave. Lucky them that they get to.

It drives me fucking crazy!

So Covid has become the 'leveller' now. It has helped reform our view of what is important, and what is not; at least to some degree. I recall in that first lockdown how quiet everything was. No sound of cars rushing by, or the distant drone of planes overhead. The air seemed to grow sweeter and I enjoyed being wheeled into the garden, and spending hours outdoors. I would stare up at the sky and wonder at the sheer unnatural silence. It was almost the kind of silence that snow brings. After a few weeks I would swear that the natural world seemed to refill the air with the sweet scents of grass, flowers and tree blossom.

Everyone was saying how much more you could hear bird song, now that they were no longer drowned out by all the usual human-made noises of engines and such-like.

I kind of wondered if that was entirely accurate, or the whole picture at least. It occurred to me that they birds were singing as much in relief that the world seemed to have tilted slightly, and humans seemed no longer in charge, or clumping around in their heavy work boots, trampling all of the good stuff in their wake as anything else. It was a time for reflection for me, and whilst I could say that about every day - as that is all I can do now - for some reason the year of Covid made me feel ever so slightly less alone.

Ever so very slightly...

17

Rage

Today the rage is huge. It feels like a forest fire, or an earthquake; the size of which is unimaginable. I am filled with fury and hatred towards the world of humans. I feel sick and confused, small and powerless. All at once. There is no real indication as to why...except the bleedin' obvious. The wind just seemed to pick up, then changed direction, and like those dark, tall, spiralling twisters that you sometimes see in american news reports, it started winding its way across the country, ripping up trees and folding massive barns, as if they were made of paper. It just started.

I woke up as normal, and even felt pretty okay in myself for a change. I waited until mom and dad got up, and listened as they moved downstairs and into the kitchen. I pictured dad putting the kettle on, and mom getting the milk out of the fridge, then moving to where she keeps the pots and pans.

Tuesdays are nearly always porridge days in the winter. Well, most days are porridge days for me due to the need for spoon feeding *'safe foods'* to ensure that I don't choke.

Then, after about five minutes, there is a light tap on my bedroom door, and I hear either mom, or dad asking if they can come in. The futility of that gesture has a different effect on me according to my mood. If I am feeling okay, I smile inwardly at the foolishness of expecting me to be able to shout, 'come in.' On the dark days (like today) I feel the desire to roll away from the doorway, and stare at the wall. But that small act is not even possible without my having to be assisted. On those days I usually spend my time wanting to lash out. Not just at my family, but also my friends...well, pretty much everyone on the whole fucking planet truth be told!

On those days there is little sign of Callum, he is replaced by this immobile force that wishes the world would just end. That all of the fucking selfish, power-hungry cunts, who seek to have power would just launch their missiles, or release whatever virus they have stashed away deep underground in some innocous looking tiny vials and be done with it. Once and for all.

I lay in my bed, or sit propped in my wheelchair as the fury boils the very blood in my veins. I aim it at anyone and everyone. I don't discriminate. The idiots who park their cars way up on the pavement, so that wheelchair users have to bounce down steep curbs just to get around them, irrespective of whether or not the road is narrow, or too busy to be safe. I rail at all the people who throw their litter into the bushes, or down on the ground, blind to the fact that nobody is coming along to pick up after them. Grown 'adults' who are able to carry their can of beer, or cider whilst there is still some left, but as soon as that last drop is gone they hurl it over a wall, or into a rail-siding. Out of sight, out of mind eh?

Cunts, the lot of them.

At times I hate everything. Even the sound of my own breathing. Yeah, sometimes that is the worst sound of all, as that is the one thing that I never want to hear again. I want that sound to be the last thing that I ever hear. If there is any kind of after-life, then I am guessing they don't allow, or have wheelchairs, or hoists, or bath-lifts, or fucking lousy raised toilet seats designed for the hoist-user. Oh yeah, in case I forgot to mention it, the house is now slowly filling up with all the necessary adaptations for me, for my wheelchair, my special bed and pressure relieving mattress (a recent purchase, that one) as the skin on my buttocks, and around the upper parts of my thighs is now breaking down, worse than ever. The only irony there...I cannot feel a thing. I cannot shake the feeling that someday, pretty soon though, I will start to smell it...and the notion fills me with disgust. Wait! Amend that to, 'fills me with even greater self disgust' at what I have become. Yes, I mean *what* too, as I no longer feel human.

So I repeat, I don't know when I stopped feeling okay and when I started to feel angry. Not today anyway. It seemed to turn up announced, and simply pulled up a chair right by the side of my bed. And when mom came into the room with my breakfast on a tray, the coffee safely decanted into a beaker with a little spout that allows me to drink without spilling hot fluid on myself, the rage springs up and offers the chair to my mother. It turns a look on me of pure glee, and my heart turns to stone. My eyes, being the only window into how I am feeling are burning hot, and I so badly want to scream, 'get out....why can't you just leave me the fuck alone?' But I can't. And knowing that only pours oil onto the flames.

I lay there, glaring at my poor mother, hating that she can stand up. Hating that she is still fully functioning. Just hating.

'Cal,' she says, hesitantly, 'do you want me to come back later?'

At that one small act of kindness and pure insight my mood suddenly changes direction, and I find myself crying. Not tears of frustration or rage, but tears of such total and all encompassing grief at everything that has been lost to me. I feel them hot and wet, tracking down my cheeks and my body is racked with huge sobs that seem to come from the very centre of my being.

Mom scoops me into her arms, crying openly herself now, and holds me tightly. I can feel her head against mine and her tears wet on the side of my neck. I won't lie. It feels good to be held, and we stay that way for what seems like hours. Two survivors of a storm that has swept away everything that we own; everything that we hold dear.

She talks to me softly, soothingly, saying that it will be alright and that things will get better...but I cannot feel those words inside me. It is like they too have been made homeless by the terrible storm, that has obliterated everything in its path. I want to feel them, and to take comfort from them, so I wrap imaginary fingers around them in my mind, and slide them into a pocket. Maybe later I will take them out and feel the weight and warmth of them against my skin.

All of a sudden it strikes me that my self pity is perhaps the cause of my rage. I refuse to spend the rest of my life feeling like a victim. I have a choice in that...if nothing else! I know that I cannot change what has happened to me. I cannot. I am told that I won't recover from what has happened. Not physically at least. No amount of physio will return movement, or even feeling to my wasted arms or legs. There is no adaptation to help me to stand upright, or to walk. Maybe one day there will be, but not right now.

My brain is the one thing that is still right as rain, and it chatters like an insane monkey. Constantly telling me all kinds of terrible things and filling my mind with dark images. Though it is much darker in there than ever before, and even the brightest lights rarely cut through the gloom that fills that one remaining, and active part of my body.

No one saves us but ourselves. No one can and no one may. We ourselves must walk the path.

Buddhist saying

18

Winter

It is the middle of February, and I feel so abjectly black inside that it is hard to think straight. I want this to stop. I think about dying all of the time at the moment. Sure, there are moments in the day when I level out, but they are few and far between. This winter seems to have lasted forever; with endless days of rain and freezing cold. I wake early, often around 4 - 5 a.m and it is still pitch black outside. I lay there in the dark, for hours on end, just waiting for some light to seep into the room. And when it does I find myself staring down at my immovable body beneath the sheets that cover me...hating.

Hating my body for its complete unwillingness to do what it was designed for. Hating it for making me feel small, useless and dependent; almost as if I was an infant again. Hating it for refusing to even allow me the dignity of speech, or to decide for myself when or how I take a pee, or worse still a fucking shit!

Hating the fact that I now have to be spoon-fed. Like a baby. That I cannot raise a hand to my mouth to feed myself, or to even cover my mouth when I cough, worse still, when I drool. Then the anger completely engulfs me, and the world simply ceases to be.

I pray to cease being, right up there with it.

When the anger recedes, it is like the aftermath of some giant tsunami that has brought earth shattering tidal waves, wiping out everything in their wake. I walk for hours, seeking human life amongst the rubble of what were towns, villages and entire cities; all now razed to the ground. Eventually, I hear a faint voice coming from inside the rubble of what is left of a house. Then I dig feverishly with my hands, until they are bleeding and raw, only to find a person barely alive, and barely conscious. Every single time, they look just like me. Every single time.

I can on occasion, view some of this with a degree of rationality....but christ that is rare! I mean, you try having your dinner cut up into small, manageable bite-sized pieces, or worse still blended; for fear that you may choke. Then sit there with a bib, or napkin tied around your neck, and accept being fed what was once your dinner as soft, warm mush and see if you don't feel like biting the hand that feeds you.

What makes that even worse (if that is even possible) is that at 26 years old it is your mother, or your father or little sister having to do it. How it feels for them I cannot even begin to imagine.

I know that my silent rage is the last thing that they need when they are also feeling pretty fucking torn up inside having to do it. I also know that those days when I am withdrawn and sullen are impossibly hard for everyone involved...but after it is done, I get to wrestle (alone) with the guilt for being this way. If I could only endure some of it with 'good grace' it might be easier on all of us...but how the hell I can achieve that I have no idea.

The very best I can do right now is try every day that I wake up...to do just that fraction better than the day before. But, the next morning on waking, I find that the depression has whipped itself into a new fury and swirls above me like a lethal gas cloud.

But what I hate most about the outline of my body beneath the bedclothes...is that it looks like me.

Or a pathetic, twisted version of the shadow of somebody I used to be.

Then, at the end of the afternoon, it is dark around 4 p.m. and it matches the way I feel...but more than that, it magnifies the way I feel. I once heard depression described as the *'dark night of the soul'* by some guy called Eckhart Tolle. I actually picked up a copy of one of his books at the local library and read it cover-to-cover in one afternoon. I think the book was called something like, *The Power of Now*. Or something like that. Anyway, I recall one entire passage, almost word-for-word, as I used some of it in a lyric for a song I wrote. Here's what Eckhart Tolle says about the dark night:

The 'dark night of the soul' is a term that goes back a long time. It's a term used to describe what one could call a collapse of a perceived meaning in life...an eruption into your life of a deep sense of meaninglessness. The inner state in some cases is very close to what is conventionally called depression. Nothing makes sense anymore, there's no purpose to anything.

Yes! That last line rings true. Most days at the moment. It is like I have fallen into a huge hole and it is so dark that I can see absolutely nothing. No outlines or shapes. I cannot even see my hand in front of my face, and moving in any direction feels too dangerous. So, I stay utterly still, and utterly terrified.

Nothing makes sense anymore, there's no purpose to anything.

19

Feelings

The tears seem never ending. It turns out that whilst most of my body is now on permanent shutdown, my emotions are sharper, and keener than I could ever have dreamed possible. So sharp in fact, that when I get too careless I cut myself. And those cuts seem to take forever to heal. The sheer range of mood-swings that I can go through moment-by-moment, and day-by-day is staggering. It feels like some of the really big waves that we used to get winter surfing in Devon, when you feel all of the breath pushed out of your lungs by the cold, dark water. I recall fighting to the surface and feeling just a tad uneasy that maybe I was out of my depth, and beyond my skill level.

Now though my useless emaciated body is washed away, and battered against the rocks, until I am bruised, bloodied and close to the end. Close, but not there quite yet there.

Christ but I wish that I were on occasion.

But the tears...well, they seem almost constant. My sadness and grief at what has happened overwhelms me, and it feels bottomless; like a well, that runs down, and down and knows no end point. I find that some days I am crying when I wake up from the thin, troubled and restless thing that masquerades as sleep now. I can no longer brush those tears away, but oddly that is one thing that I no longer care about. Or wish to do. It is a blessed relief (if those are the right words) to be able to physically feel them, as I feel so little else.

There are other physical feelings and sensations still, even with my condition, like choking, coughing and sometimes even breathing. All of those utterly natural functions that we all take for granted are now a risk, that before the accident I would never have imagined possible. I am told that I am lucky not to have a Tracheostomy, which is essentially a hole in the neck to breathe through. What is that expression, *'Thank heavens, for small mercies'* is it? Yeah, that sounds about right. But to me, it also sounds like a sick joke!

Go tell it to someone else though why don't you?

How the fuck is a person to cry when they cannot even breathe properly? It seems to me that God, the universe, the IS -

call it whatever you like - is infinitely cruel. Oh, I know, that isn't reasonable of me to believe such a thing, but life isn't always fair, and it sure as hell isn't reasonable at times. When you think about all of those stupid phrases and aphorisms that we peddle from time-to-time, to make people feel better, or more comfortable, like *'even bad things happen to good people,'* and '*be careful what you wish for,'* and maybe you wouldn't disagree with me.

Again, I guess that I am straying away from the path of my thoughts...well, feelings anyway. But one last little phrase, 'big boys don't cry.' Well I am here to tell you that I beg to differ. Yes they fucking well do! And not without good reason either. There is an old song covered by a whole bunch of artists, called *Cry me a River*, that suggests otherwise. I recall trying to learn it on the guitar for a girlfriend at school. I was searching for the chords on the web, and found an article that said that it was written by an artist called Julie London in 1955. The song itself was actually written for a show starring Ella Fitzgerald, but it was dropped and Ella didn't record her version of it until a few years later. Loads of great singers have covered it since, most notably Barbra Streisand. And she is one old-school female artist that I have always kinda loved. There is something so classy, smart, sexy, and unique about her. Hmm, maybe there is a closet gay man inside of me after all.

Who knows?

The hardest thing about this rollercoaster of emotions is not being able to talk about them with anyone. If there was ever any doubt that talking therapies have some kind of efficacy, then I am here to say that 'yes' they sure do. I can say that with unshakeable belief as not being able to tell people just how I feel, makes every day that much harder, and at times I even fear that the sheer levels of my rage, depression and sadness will overwhelm me completely, and I feel like I will split open like a ripe fruit.

What people don't realise is that our ability to talk is for the very purpose of communicating how we are feeling, as well as all manner of other things. Whilst there is only a certain percentage of spoken language that conveys meaning, and the rest is the nuances of body language, tone of voice, facial features etc...even some of those areas are lost to me now.

If you asked me if I feel lonely. Well, there I likely would be speechless for a while...lost for the words that could adequately describe the scope of my feelings...even if I were able to communicate verbally. Loneliness is a physical weight now. It bears down on me day-in and day-out, crushing the thin breath from my lungs.

And yes, I know that we have all been through the whole Covid 19 thing over the last year or so, which is one of the most unique experiences in the last hundred years or so, but loneliness has many faces. Not just that of being physically alone. It has multiple masks that it can pick and choose from dependent on how it feels, and which way the wind is blowing. It subtly alters its course by the winds, and barely perceptible pressure changes. It can make tiny adjustments by the time of day, or the changing of the seasons. It knows no language barriers, or boundaries and it can pick any lock that it pleases.

There is nowhere to hide from loneliness.

Nowhere at all.

20

Troubled

I am deeply troubled by two major things at the moment. The first thing is the sheer amount of time on my hands doing nothing. The other thing is the almost complete lack of control, sway, or influence that I have over almost everything that happens to me, and around me. And both of those issues feed off each other too, like starving vultures. They fight for the tastiest pieces of meat, and screech at anything, or anyone who comes close.

The time issue I can do nothing about. It affects all of us. Human society marks and keeps time like it is some precious thing to be saved, hidden away and cherished. Yet we cannot hold it in our hands. Time has become my enemy. There it is written down. It is an inarguable, immutable fact. I have started to wonder how I shall survive each day if I can do nothing. Let's face it, most people *do* something. Most of the time in fact. We have school, college, university, jobs, friends and a social life. We go to theatres, cinemas, bars, clubs, restaurants, pubs, gigs and festivals. When we come home at night at whatever time, and we flop down into a comfortable armchair, or sofa. Or better still bed. And we do nothing. We've earned it.

And there is the real rub you see. You earn getting to *do nothing*, therefore you get to really enjoy it, to savour it like a good meal, or a fine glass of wine. Take out the activity and why would you need to flop down onto a couch and do nothing? Would it feel as good? What would you get from it? And here is the bigger question, do you deserve it?

You would likely feel as I do, that you don't. You are not filling your life with anything worthwhile...or to put it more accurately, you are not *fulfilling your life*. How am I to feel fulfilled when I am doing nothing? When I can do nothing!

The hours feel like days, and the days feel like weeks. They stretch ahead of me, far off into the distance in hideous mockery. After a while the days and weeks all start to blend into one. You lose all track of time (no bad thing) and it doesn't matter what day of the week it is. They all look and feel the same. The *colour* that should fill our lives start to fade, and eventually reality becomes monochrome. And when you get that far, you find yourself sliding inexorably towards the abyss. Then rapidly the slide becomes a gravitational pull, and you pick up speed before giving up all hope.

Then disappear over the edge. As I have.

I am not about to give up though. Don't get me wrong, but it is hard to not feel like a ghost in a world that is all about movement, activity and sound. I feel as if I move between these worlds unseen now, as each energy no longer emanates from me. I am a study in silence, stillness and inactivity. I have become a phantom. A silent watcher of the world. And I am no longer even a part of it.

I truly believe that to see the splendour in life, we have to be out there, *in it.* We have to immerse ourselves fully and not worry about drowning. Life is not lived being cooped up, day-after-day in a house filled with gadgets and adaptations, just waiting for the next soft meal.

Now we come to my second point, or bone of contention. My inability to communicate. I want you to try to get yourself into my head and into my shoes...much use they are to me! Take your time and have a good think about what it is like to not be able to ask for what you need. Okay. Not having a voice is one thing. There are people without hearing, or the power of speech and they still play a valuable role in society.

But now take away the ability to simply point to the desired object, or to be able to pick up a pad and paper, and write it down, then pass it to the person helping them.

What is left? Sure, we can look at the object, or the door that leads to the room that holds the object, or signify the activity, or need that we have, but then you have to rely on the interpretation of the *listener*. What if they pick up completely the wrong signal and start wheeling towards the toilet, or away from the kitchen, or object you desire, when all the while all you wanted was for them to wipe your runny nose?

How would you stop and correct them? Okay, we have facial gestures, I will give you that. In fact quite a large percentage of our communication and understanding of each other is made up of all of the subtle nuances that underpin what we say, think and feel. I am guessing now that most of the time we take for granted. the combination of facial gestures, tone of voice, physical prompts, eye contact etc. Imagine what it would be like to be blind then. How much would we miss out then? All of those infinitesimally small, valuable little signals and gestures that serve to help us to communicate fully.

I am left wondering again, why the really important aspects of our humanity are invisible. By that I mean everything that we think, feel and even all of our needs. Then it strikes me, and I feel my mood dip even lower.

That is why we have the power of speech.

21

Ghosts

'When the room is quiet. The daylight almost gone

It seems there's something I should know.

Well, I ought to leave but the rain it never stops

And I've no particular place to go'

At this point in the story of anyone's life, there has to be some reason behind the telling...but I cannot find one, and the result is that I am lost. I have become a ghost to all intents and purposes, and ghosts do not have stories. At least not beyond how they died. Nor do they have people to tell them to. And they most certainly don't have a purpose. Other than haunting the living anyway. Maybe the haunting is a direct consequence of no longer being able to tell their story, or make a discernible mark on a world that no longer sees them.

Why all this talk of ghosts I suppose you are wondering. Well, I guess it came into my mind during those interminable long winter's evenings when I would lay in bed, from late afternoon through the evening, when having taken some food, and done the necessary personal care I would find myself lowered into bed, and have even more hours of darkness. Physical darkness and internal, if I am honest. It led me to remembering that as a child I was scared of the dark. I may have mentioned that earlier on, but cannot for the life of me be sure.

The dark seemed to me to be like a living breathing entity. It filled up my lungs, and forced the breath out of me. I was helpless and simply terrified to be left alone in it. As I got older that changed at some point, quite naturally. I don't recall when, or how, or even why, but it did. I moved on to find new things to distract me I suppose. New passions and teenage interests came bounding into my life, and some of the fears of childhood just upped and left. No great fuss made. No fanfare, or leaving card. They just packed up their few meagre belongings and let themselves out the back door.

I guess that our fears are rather like ghosts, they move on to haunt the next owner of the house, or they wander the moors for eternity, wailing and moaning, and clanking their heavy chains. They come to us late at night when sleep won't, and they warn us of what may come, if we don't amend our wicked ways. Oh, I know that's a rather overly dramatic, Dickensian image, but forgive me if my reference is not Scrooge from the classic Christmals Carol story, but from Scrooged, the classic Bill Murray film. I am a young guy, and such things have an influence. My life now is a lot like his. Every day is pretty much a carbon copy of the one before it. I have my routines, and naturally they have to fit in around mom and dad's schedules and Melissa's too. I worry that there will come a point when they cannot manage my needs and then what? That thought has the sharpest teeth of all.

Since the accident, I have new fears. These ones don't come drifting through the walls like apparitions late at night when everyone is asleep. No, these ones appear anytime they damn well please. Day or night. These ones have much louder voices and sharper teeth, and nails that they rake down your back, leaving bright red trails of blood in their wake.

They have names too. Big names like muscle atrophy, urinary tract infections, muscle spasticity and sepsis. Well, not all of them are big names, but let's not split hairs. Believe me when I tell you that when words like that are used in relation to you, they scare the living fucking daylights out of you, and you find yourself wishing that you were just afraid of the dark. Or maybe the sound a person makes when they run their nails down a blackboard. Oh yes, there are worse things than ghosts I can tell you.

I am happier laying in the dark now than I have ever been. I prefer it in fact, if the truth be told. It suits how I feel on the inside a lot of the time. The dark never gives me migraines like bright lights and sometimes even daylight does either. So in some ways, it has become a friend to me. I lay there listening to the whispering inside me and feel like I am a ghost. I stare into the darkness and imagine that I am whole, and that none of this nightmare is happening.

At those times, I feel free. Free from the terrible restraints of my body, from reality, this room, this planet and from having to feel. It is blissful to be rid of the angst, the sadness, the anger and the shame. To watch as it melts away and there is a silence within me, that is comforting and real. Even if these moments are fleeting, I look forward to them, and embrace them.

It feels like coming home.

Well, I'm feeling nervous, now I find myself alone

The simple life's no longer there

Once I was so sure, now the doubt inside my mind

Comes and goes but leads nowhere

Ghosts - Japan

22

What?

'So, what is the going rate for a cripple nowadays?'

I woke up with that thought clanging around in my head this morning, and the first thing that I saw was that it was raining. Hard. It looks freezing cold, and it is coming down in almost translucent sheets. For a split second I could almost see myself standing outside, feeling the prick and sting of the rain as it hit my head, face and shoulders. The cold biting deeply into my raw skin as it saturated my clothes would feel like a blessing to me. I could picture, quite vividly, the shards of water as they bounced and shimmered off my body.

My upright and whole body.

I lay there, in my bed and let the sadness come. It crept towards me, timid at first, but then with eager relish as it caught sight of my well known face, and recognised its host...the cripple in the bed.

And then the thought came, hard on the heels of sadness...*what is the going rate for a cripple nowadays?* What am I worth now to society? Do I have a role, or function anymore? Apart from taking up a small amount of space, and being a constant burden to my family and a source of bitter guilt (quite likely) to some of my friends.

Who was it who said, 'I think, therefore I am?' Was it Descartes, or Freud? I am not sure...but then realise that the source of the quote is kind of immaterial. I might think, but then I am still not going to amount to much. Nor am I likely to *do* much with my life now. If indeed *doing*, is the only true measure of a person's worth, and as a male of the species, I sure enjoyed always having something to do, and being engaged with the flow of life. It was true to say that I rarely sat still for very long. Then suddenly it occurred to me. If I can still be physically seen, then at least I am real. *I am visible, therefore I am*, would seem more accurate then...wouldn't it? At that thought, I became aware that for the first time since the accident there was a very subtle change - or lift - in my mood. I felt, very slightly lighter of spirit. I have wondered for most of the last year about my worth, in one way or another, and had not come up with anything concrete. Unless that is self-hatred has a purpose, or a currency.

I had pondered on the notion that if a person makes music, writes a book, or creates art and nobody listens, or reads, or listens...then is there any point? I kept coming up with the clear, and loud answer NO! No point at all. It seemed that whilst there is pleasure for the author, artist or musician in the ideas, and the creation of their art, for it to be fully realised and to truly earn its right to a life of its own, then it needs to be *experienced* by others. The extrapolation of that line of thinking though, is that if I can still be seen (or experienced), then I still matter. In fact I am still *matter*, of a sort. Physical matter anyway. Sure, I don't move so well, and I am not about to stand up and sing Streets of Philadelphia out loud, but I am still taking up space in this world and I can still think!

Christ....whoever thought up the line, *'I think, therefore I am,'* was right. I still *am.*

My thoughts were interrupted by a tentative knock on my bedroom door and I smiled ever so slightly, as I heard my little sister's voice asking if she could come in. She opened the door and stepped hesitantly into the room. She was wearing her kimono style dressing gown and her usual fluffy, open toed slippers; the ones with the goofy looking dachshund faces on them. I looked into her eyes and felt my smile turn into a grin. Hell, but that felt good. I could not recall the last time that I had smiled. Not fully anyway.

'What are you smiling at big brother?' She asked, now grinning at me like a Cheshire cat herself and sliding herself onto my bed to give me a hug....that for once, I would actually allow myself to enjoy.

I couldn't answer her. Naturally. But even if there was nothing wrong with my voice, I am not sure I could have answered. Not out loud anyway, as all of a sudden I felt like crying. But not from sadness. More from a sense of joy that I suddenly felt welling up inside of me. Looking back, I realise that my smile was enough of an answer.

It was a start at least.

23

Perspective

A friend of mine came to visit me today. I have known him pretty much my whole life. We went to the same primary school it turns out. I didn't really get to know him then, as we didn't share any classes together, and I went to a different secondary school for two years, where my grades dipped alarmingly (I had discovered music and girls) and my parents shifted me to the same school as him. I was relieved he was there as I only knew two people in the whole damn place, and the first day was pretty scary I seem to recall.

Anyway, his name is Phil and we are really close. I was his best man at his wedding and even agreed to wear a suit, something I am not given to doing - given the choice!

He sat by the side of my wheelchair, as I was up and in the lounge that day. He was telling me about his wife's grandfather who had lost his wife about five years ago, to Cancer. It turns out that the old guy had suffered some strokes and was pretty much confined to bed. He lived alone, and insisted it stay that way. He wanted nothing to do with going into a nursing or residential home, and the rest of the family had respected his wishes...even though he needed help to move, eat, manage personal care etc. Sound like anyone we know?

Phil was saying that he was going over there later that day to take him his meds and see if he needed anything. He went on to say that 'Pops' as they all called him, was also demented to some degree, but to what degree was not clear. Apparently he greets Phil by name and asks him how he is. I sat there listening, desperately wondering if the old guy knew who Phil actually was...in context I mean, as his son-in-law, or whether he just recognised the face and could add at least the right name to it.

I wanted to ask him questions, and became more and more frustrated that I could not. All I had managed in terms of communication was to move my eyes. Sure, that worked if I needed something, as I could look at it if it was an object, or in the direction of the bathroom, if I wanted to shower, or outside if I needed air, but true, connected conversation felt a million miles away.

I pushed the thoughts away and tried to focus on what Phil was saying as he went on to say that he had known the old guy only a couple of years, but how amazing it was that he was 'happy' alone, every single day, with only a couple of family members coming in every other day, and carers coming in three times a day. What occurred to me initially was that he must be out of his mind, or at least going out of his mind....but then Phil said something that grabbed my full attention. He said something like, 'the old guy was always pretty lazy, and never much for talking and was pretty much happy in his own little world.' He said more than that but that was the rough jist of it. He carried on talking, telling me about his little sister who had just got married, but I admit that I wasn't really listening. I had fixated on what he said about Phil's grandfather-in-law, if that is the right term.

He talked for about fifteen minutes or so, then stood up to leave saying he would pop in for the football and the boxing on Saturday. Phile liked watching boxing for some reason. I didn't, but I always appreciated the company. When he had gone I 'asked' mom, who reads my eye movement better than anyone, if I could go back to my room. I was tired but I lay there for a good while watching as the clouds spun lazily past outside my window. *Lazy. Lazy.* The words, like the clouds drifted back into my mind constantly. Was that how the old guy had survived then? Was it in his very nature to be happy alone, and seemingly unstimulated?

All I could know however is that whilst our circumstances were scarily similar, we were at the opposite ends of the age spectrum and I still had my family around me. I had to figure that the old guy was likely late 80's now, and I was only 26 years old. We were both house-bound, and virtually bed-bound, or he was at least; yet he chose that life, and I still deep down wanted more from my life!

At that thought, I found that I felt something inside of me stir again and get added to the little reserve of desire that was now burning brightly. At first it had been just like the soft glow of a candle in the dark, that flickered in the slight breeze that blew through from time-to-time. But now the flame was burning just that little bit brighter and hotter. It was the start of something. It was the start of a new perspective.

Quite where that perspective would lead me I had no idea, but it was a fine replacement for the darkness of depression, anger and an aching longing for death. As I slid into a soft, dreamless sleep my last thought was to wonder what I could still *do* that would bring me fully back to life. I accepted that I didn't know.

Not yet.

24

Eyes

I was troubled after Phil left and lay on my bed wondering whether there was some way in which I could get back to *talking* in some way again. I had some faint memory of my specialist talking about speech and language therapy but had dismissed the notion once it became clear that I would have no actual, out loud speech capability. I so badly wanted to be able to interact with people again, and to be able to express my needs, thoughts and emotions. I felt like I would erupt if I didn't find a way of doing so. But...how in hell was I going to communicate even that need? How?

There is a saying, 'when the pupil is ready, the master appears.' It seems my dad is indeed a master, of sorts as right out of the blue, only the very next day did he quietly enter my room, sit down on the bed and fan out an array of brochures all displaying technology for people to communicate using only their eyes.

'You've been at home for a fair few months now Cal and we all agree that we would like to hear from you more often,' he said in that quiet, matter-of-fact way that he has. I looked up at him with a huge lump in my throat. I would love to say that I was lost for words at this point...but it wasn't words that I was lost for. I had those, all racing around in my head, but the loudest thing in the room at that moment was my gratitude and love for this quiet, unassuming man who sat in front of me.

I struggle to express the level of gratitude and relief that flooded through me in that moment. I have never felt more loved, more visible or more cherished than I did in that moment. That he had quietly gone about researching all of the possible ways in which he could open up the channels of communication and then just wandered into my room, not making any fuss, was staggering to me. I always knew that my father was a man who needed no fanfare, no spotlight, or big fusses made over the things that he did, but this floored me. Tears of relief, gratitude, sadness and happiness streamed down my face. He simply lifted a work roughened hand and wiped them away.

'It's okay son,' he said. His voice with its deep Scottish brogue slightly thicker than usual. I saw a tear slip from the corner of one eye, and seeing that made my cry even harder. He put both of his arms around me and lifted me gently into a bear hug. I could smell his cologne and the clean smell of his hair. It was a familiar and welcome smell that always made me feel safe. It was the smell of my father. Unique, safe, warm and comforting. People get inside our hearts, and that is one of the best things about being human...being loved.

I have never understood why simple acts of kindness affect me in the way that they do...but understanding everything is overrated in my opinion. Sometimes we just have to accept things as they are.

We sat there for nearly two hours reading the brochures. He turned the pages as I read. From what we could tell it seemed that the whole package that I would require to give me back complete control of my PC or laptop, and be able to use the speech function would be no more than about £4,500. I was pretty staggered by that as I had been anxious that it would be more like seven to ten grand in all. I recall grinning for the rest of the day. It was a really special and quiet few hours with my father and I will never forget it for as long as I live.

Never.

The technology it seemed, utilises the movement of the eyes instead of touch. Imagine that instead of a physical keyboard that you tap away at with your fingers, you simply look into a camera and it 'reads' the movement of your gaze. So essentially, you look at an on-screen keyboard, and choose the letter, or phrase, or number, or instruction that you want.

I could, should I so desire (and if money were no object) operate all the systems in the house. Like the heating, the lights, the TV, radio etc. but we figured I wouldn't need to control the house as mom, dad and little sis had the pretty much covered. All we needed to do was to find the right product, and apparently the set up is pretty quick. It's rather like calibrating a voice activated keyboard in your mobile phone. The only difference is that I have no voice. But think about it, the eyes are referred to as the '*windows of the soul.*' There is something quite poetic about it eh? Every eye is unique in its make-up too, I found out by Googling it once. It said something like this;

'The iris is a ring-shaped membrane located behind the cornea of the eye. It is responsible for controlling how much light enters the eye. The colour and structure of the iris are determined by your DNA, but the pits, rifts, furrows, and swirls of the iris are different in every individual. This makes every iris unique'

Nice eh? It's rather like our fingerprints in that regard. So, it was a no-brainer that set up the software to recognise my eyes, and their movements would be pretty quick. The excitement that I felt was huge. I simply couldn't wait to order it and get it set up. By the end of the day, we had selected about four providers in all. Dad got up off the bed and went and got his mobile from the lounge, and he called and spoke with three of them in all as it was coming up 5 o'clock and so we waited until the next morning to speak with the fourth provider.

We decided to go with a British-based organisation up north, just as they seemed really switched on and friendly on the phone. There were american companies and a Swedish one too if my memory serves me right. The provider we opted for also had the best priced equipment, and dad was impressed not only with the amazing warmth of the people working for the small company, but also their efficiency. When they said they would call straight back, they did so. When they said they would send things through the post straight away, we received the article the very next day.

In the space of one week we had everything that we needed. And get this, all-in the cost for the whole package was less than £4,150. I was happy to pay for the whole damned shooting match but mom and dad pulled a fast one and paid the 'deposit' as they referred to it, of £2,000. I suspected that to not be the entire truth as how asking for that much money for anything other than a car, or something? Again I found myself in tears, so profoundly grateful at the sheer level of selflessness and kindness that they had for me. I sat in my wheelchair weeping quietly until little sis sat right next to me and wrapped her arms around me. That sure didn't make it any less overwhelming and we all sat that way for about 15 minutes, the whole family crying. Mom and dad clinging to each other like survivors on a life raft.

What a picture it would have made.

Once all of the gear arrived it didn't take more than a few hours to set up, as once we had figured out how to set up the tripod that the screen sits on, which can also be adjusted to my seating, or lying position we were pretty much good to go. Not to mention the fact that all of the software and configuration work was all done before it was even posted to us.

I was kinda relieved that the software wasn't (at that time) compatible with Apple software as their stuff is generally an arm and a leg in terms of cost.

Christ...the irony of my using that phrase isn't lost on me...

Oh, the name of the technology by the way is Eye Gaze. I have no idea who created it, but I thank whichever god's in charge of IT for its existence. If this were the seventies, or sixties, I would just be a person in a bed with no ability to reach around the world via the internet, or turn up the heating without getting someone else to do it for me. You know how much it all cost? Not as much as I thought initially but I think by the time I had everything I needed, it was less than £6,000. Not bad when you consider an Apple laptop is over £2,000 nowadays. I didn't mind using some of the money that I had saved from my old tree-surgery job, as it was always intended to be spent on one form of freedom or another. And yes, being able to talk or communicate may not seem like a *freedom* to you, but believe me when I say that it sure is to me.

If that concept seems odd, just stop and think about it. How free is a person locked inside a box? Unable to move, or make decisions, interact with others, go shopping, or even take a walk outside. It can be an end to travel, work, new experiences, love, relationships. Put like that it even occurs to me that a close second is surely prison, and who generally sees a human body as a form of prison? Now there is something to think about.

It's funny, we used to do a cover of an old song by Gary Numan called 'I dream of wires.' The lyrics went something like this:

'We opened doors by thinking.
We went to sleep by dialing 'O'.
We drove to work by proxy.
I plugged my wife in, just for show.'

The words of that song always made me smile whenever we performed it live, and how prophetic the words seem to me now, just a few short months later. I won't exactly be opening doors by thinking, but it is not exactly a million miles wide of the mark, and I am sure that I heard or read somewhere that what used to be referred to as *Science Fiction*, is now often called *Science*

Faction. We are constantly moving forwards in so many areas of science, and with technology now able to give me access and visibility in the world of humans again...it sure makes a whole heap of sense eh? The only difference here is the use of the words *I dream of wires* in the lyrics, as they seem to be becoming less and less present in our day-to-day lives.

I know that I am straying from the topic here but whilst I am on the subject of Gary Numan, I became a bit of a closet fan when I was in my late teens, having seen some footage of him on YouTube performing some songs from a new album that he had just released. Initially I liked his more recent stuff, which is quite dark, and really heavy, Which is definitely right up my street. Then dad played me some of his earlier albums, from the eighties where he had just crossed over from being a guitar-based punk band to the whole synthesizer sound that took the eighties by storm. It was a case of love at first hearing again, and I just about wore out the three albums that dad still had on vinyl. It seems he was (and still is, I believe) quite obsessed with technology and many of his earlier songs are about a future world where humans are no longer in control.

There is a one song called, Down in the Park, that has a line that goes, *'Oh look there's a rape machine. I'd go outside if it would look the other way. You wouldn't believe the things they do.'* That struck me as brilliant. Pretty funny too. That we would finally usurp ourselves, and even end up afraid of the things that we built, which no longer want or need us to survive and thrive.

Sometimes, I cannot help wondering if the human race will actually go that far with our constant messing about with science and nature. And what would stop us from doing so? We don't seem to learn terribly quickly, or very well when it comes to building, or creating things that in hindsight don't serve humanity. The opposite is often true in fact and we have enough weapons to incinerate the whole planet now...just in case we should ever need to. And, who I wonder is keeping an eye on us? Rather like children, we could do with an authority much greater than our own, to remind us from time-to-time to go wash our hands, quiet down and come sit up at the table.

Maybe that is why we invented God. Or was that the other way around?

25

Love

It may seem odd, the heading of this chapter. Especially coming straight after my telling you all about my new found technology and how it has helped me to return to the world of interaction. Beyond eye-blinking, scowling and rolling my eyes anyway. There is a reason why it has to go in here. And that reason is that since finding my voice (well, a generic computer generated one anyway) I feel very different. The dark clouds of depression and hopelessness seem far, far away in the distance. Sometimes, if you listen very closely you can hear the low rumble of thunder, and if you squint then you might just catch the odd flash of lightning on the horizon. Rarely though does it roll back across the plains towards you, and certainly nowhere near as frequently as it has over the last year or so.

It is a huge relief and an almost unnatural joy to be able to actually respond to something that is said to me. Imagine telling a joke and nobody ever laughs, or playing tennis with someone who never, ever hits the ball back. Both would seem pretty pointless and I suspect that you would give up, and walk away muttering under your breath. Oh, with the tennis analogy you would need an endless supply of balls too. It felt like that when I was completely locked-in. For me, just as likely as it did for the people around me. I couldn't blame people for running short of conversation around me as without the ball actually coming back over the net, you might as well go talk to a wall. Maybe hit some tennis balls off of it too, whilst you are there.

I say it again, to be able to actually interact is so, so exciting to me now.

Once again I am able to ask for things that I need, to be able to tell people when my nose itches maddeningly. But one of the biggest pleasures is being able to ask how someone else is. You would not believe how disabling it is not to be able to simply ask if someone is okay. Especially when 95% of the time they would be, if only they didn't have to look after my needs constantly. It is nice to acknowledge the presence and preciousness of my family and friends again. The only problem now though is that I find that I want to talk all of the damned time. Pretty soon I reckon my family will start paying me to simply shut the hell up!

The question is still out there though as to why I have entitled this chapter Love. We all have an image, or idea of what love looks and feels like. I am sure that you, like me, have watched Hollywood films and listened to love songs, and read about it in books. But none of that is real life. Films show us a romanticised version of how it can be, to give us hope and to take us outside of ourselves for a few hours. Maybe for some people it really is like that. You read, and see on the TV these older people holding hands and telling the interviewer how they met 50-60 years ago and they are as in love today as fiercely as the day they met. That is amazing, and never fails to bring a tear to my eye, but are they the exception to the rule? Did they discover something that few of us are likely to ever find? Rather like faith, religion, or spirituality we need to believe in something in order to survive and to keep us moving forwards.

I cannot say (and wouldn't flatter myself to even try) if that kind of love is achievable for everyone; if only we worked hard at it, or had some magic dust to sprinkle over it, but I suspect that it is not for most of us. It is an idealised form that makes for good reading, or good viewing. In real life, some of us get the girl or boy...but many others never do. If you are smart, and paying attention to life, like me, maybe you will agree that one size does not fit all. Nor should it!

So, if you are wondering why a chapter on love, when I am clearly admitting to not have all of the answers then I will simply say that to realise, and understand what the true meaning of the word means to me....well, I would smile and say that I have learned the true meaning of what love means by falling out of a tree.

I guess that puts a relatively unique perspective on the phrase, to fall in love.

26

Perfect

There is something good that comes from everything. Is that inarguable truism applied to humans, do you think? I mean we have had plenty of wars throughout a fairly short existence. Does something good come from those? We have seen race riots recently in the states. Does something good come from those? Or, does it fuel an inner disgust for ourselves that we cannot quite see, but know is there and it starts to slowly infect everything in its wake?

We have had wave after wave (admittedly rather small ones) of new age movements, and new forms of therapy, meditations, books on 'new ways of being' and self-help etc. But again, why no massive changes in the collective human consciousness? Is it that we simply cannot learn from previous generations, or is it that in truth, we simply cannot learn from other people's experiences? I believe it to be the latter.

Sure, we can read history books, and there is a generally held belief that history teaches and informs future (and hopefully) current generations. And maybe it does. But how quickly and how much? It seems to me that in the last 100 years or so we have come a long way in terms of equalities in many, many countries around the world. At the same time, the divide between the truly rich, and the truly poor has widened and become a staggeringly huge gulf. We still see countries suffering terrible famines. And poverty sure looks to me like it has some comfortable footholds in a large part of this 'civilised' world that we all live in.

I want to suggest though that perhaps we inhabit more than one world. Sure we are all visible enough wandering around in our bodies, creating all sorts of merry hell...but what about the inner world that we all inhabit too? I believe that *place* is unique to each and every one of us? The outer world just holds activity, and sets of physical day-to-day patterns, routines and behaviours that we must all comply to. It sets rules and regulations to ensure that we don't get too out of hand. And then we have a safe template to refer to as we go about our business.

Or do we get to set them?

Until that is, something comes along that breaks that pattern. Like my fall. That day changed not only my life but many preconceptions that I had about life, and my place in it. I guess that it changed my family's lives too. It didn't just stop me from moving my limbs, but it changed how I was 'seen' as well. How I was treated also got altered. How could I possibly contribute anything confined to a wheelchair and a room filled with gadgets? What was my *worth?* And right there is the biggest question of all. Who does the judging as to whether we are worthwhile? And on what criteria? I had the next sentence as, *'Surely we can also be judged by what we take away from life too. No?'* But on re-reading it I saw a big hole running right through it. Why on earth am I suggesting that there is a judgement at all? Apart from our own. It is only us that asks all of these needless questions and it is only ourselves stacking up reasons to be less than perfect. It is only ourselves keeping score.

Some people suggest or believe they know that the final judgement comes from God. But isn't it a little too late by then? To live fully we must do it right now. Every single waking moment! I tried my best and for a guy who doesn't get around so well anymore I reckon I have done pretty darned okay. You see, what you are reading now is my gift to the world. My legacy. Not only to the big, wide outer one, but also to the inner one. The one where every single living breathing human is utterly and completely equal. There is no religion, or belief system, or set of rules, or politenesses here in the Inner World. We are just us. Just as we were born.

Pretty much perfect.

27

Infected

I recognise the lights above me and the sound of a siren is loud in my ears. No, not a line from a Clash or Green Day song, but me strapped to a gurney in the back of an ambulance. It seems that I may have pneumonia. I am struggling (more than normal) to breathe, and as a person who cannot move is liable to all sorts of infections, it has quickly taken hold of my body and I am falling again, tumbling over and over whilst my weak body slowly gives itself over to huge, crashing waves of infection. The only positive is that this time I won't hit the ground.

My immune system is poor to say the very least. How could it be otherwise, as the body needs to move to develop and maintain not only muscle tone, but all the other good stuff that goes with it. The only thing that moves with me I'm afraid is my mind, to quote the old Buddhist adage.

Huh, maybe I am the living embodiment of enlightenment eh?

As we careen once again through streets that I cannot see, my mind turns to one of the many articles that I read on the risks presenting to people like me, who may contract pneumonia. I know, a bit morbid, but I have been concerned that I haven't felt right over the last week or so, and wanted to do something proactive. *'So sue me.'* As the yanks say. Anyway, I highlighted the below and turned them into bullet points to make for easier reading. Oh, and I might have added some little comments of my own next to the 'no brainer' issues. So watch out for them.

- Prolonged periods of time lying down or sitting. This can allow fluid to accumulate in your lungs - *not much else that I can do.*
- The inability to control your respiratory tract. If you cannot cough, or swallow you're less adept at dislodging irritants or bacteria.
- Artificial respiratory devices. If not diligently cleaned, these products can accumulate dangerous bacteria that can lead to a dangerous infection - *mom's fault...ha, ha.*

And now for the list of symptoms from the very same article. Again, some of them I again make some pithy little comment on in italics.

- Difficulty or pain when swallowing - *the first one is pretty goddamn daily.*
- A fever, even if no other symptoms - *YES!*
- Coughing up green mucus - *yep.*
- Difficulty breathing when lying down or sleeping - *in what way is that much different from most days?? Saying that.... YES again. My breathing is more of a struggle.*

This all started a few days ago when I started to feel hotter and sweatier than normal. You would think that I would welcome an increase in body temperature as being so still I am cold a lot of the time. But this felt different. It's hard to explain, but it felt more like feverishness than simply too warm. So on waking yesterday morning, I did more searches on the internet whilst my little sister sat on the bed doing her university course homework. We know each other well enough to be comfortable in the silence that not being able to talk created throughout all those months before the Eye Gaze technology, but I always enjoy her occasional banter and it still feels great being able to respond with the odd quip, or sarcastic big brother put down.

I found this within minutes of my first search, and scrolling down the page I felt my heart grow cold. I know, a bit of a contradiction in terms but fear isn't a warm blanket. That is for sure. Again, I am cutting and pasting it in here rather than paraphrasing.

When Respiratory Infections Spread

When a respiratory infection spreads to another organ, the infection becomes significantly more difficult to treat. This is especially true for SCI survivors, who already struggle with decreased immunity, and who may have additional health problems. The more rapidly the infection spreads, the more easily your body can become overwhelmed. Even if the infection is promptly treated, it's possible to suffer serious and lasting organ, tissue, and muscle damage.

I looked up to see Melissa staring at me. The look on her face was one of alarm. Could she see that I was badly scared?

'What is it Callum?' She asked. A sense of urgency just creeping into her tone. 'I know that look big brother, something has you scared. What is it?'

She jumped off my bed and came over to the desk by the window, and peered over my shoulder at the laptop screen. Her lips formed a thin line as she quickly read the bullet points, then the sentence that I have just quoted. When she finished reading she stepped into my line of sight and her eyes showed real fear.

'Why are you researching this?' She asked. 'Have you been feeling unwell Cal? If you have you should have said something to me, or mom or dad.' Her look was stern and she was chewing at her bottom lip in that way that she does when she is stressed or really upset.

'I am going to get a thermometer and check your temperature, and if it is even a degree or two warmer than normal we are going to tell mom and dad okay?'

'Yes. Okay.' I responded. My computer's voice, rather like Stephen Hawking's one, has a rather robotic speaking voice, so belies no feelings, or emotions...but I was feeling plenty at that point I can tell you.

At that she left the room, heading for the main bathroom to go into the medicine cabinet there. I could hear her from where I was sitting, rooting around under the sink. In the past I would have called out 'medicine cabinet stupid' but no longer. The voice doesn't have quite the same reach as the vocal cords. Besides which, I wasn't feeling even remotely witty or funny at that precise moment.

I heard her mutter, 'bingo' and the sound of her feet on the floor as she padded quickly back into my room. 'Open wide big brother,' she said, shaking it briskly, then slipping the thermometer under my tongue in one quick, well practiced movement. We waited for what felt like an hour rather than a full minute, then she leant forward and withdrew it. Again, that tight lipped look, but this time the frown that creased her brow was all I needed to know that it was not good news.

'Fuck Cal, this is not good.' She said, startling me slightly with her use of the 'F' word. She ran from the room before I could even type my response, and I sat there feeling even more numb than usual.

28

Words

'Don't you tell me to keep my voice down. Don't you dare!' I heard my mom shouting at dad. 'He is my only son. My first born and now I have to stand by and watch as he dies? How am I to deal with that news? Do you have any clever suggestions?' At that her voice broke, and all I could hear were he muffled sobs as she threw herself into dad's arms. Sure, that last bit might just be my imagination, but I have got pretty good at reading situations without actually seeing them. I guess that mom might have just put a hanky to her mouth, but I have known them long enough, and seen enough to know that she is likely holding onto him for grim life, and crying against his shoulder.

One of the reasons is that she won't want me hearing her. She worries if she thinks I may be stressed by a situation, but my hearing has become pretty good since the accident, and even in my weakened state I am registering a lot of what is going on around me. I can also picture the younger, dark haired doctor that was there when I was being lifted from the ambulance, trying to explain my condition, and the steps that they could take to help me to feel better.

Deep down though, I have a feeling that this time it is going to be different. This time I have a weird presentiment that I won't be going home. I cannot for the life of me explain how I know that, but I do. There is a sense of knowing that has crept over me in the last few days. Oh I knew that my breathing was off in some way. But that has happened a million times over the last few years, and I have come to accept that I would generally need a subtle change to my medication, or to have to sleep sitting up, or be taken into hospital for some long named procedure. This though is the end of the line for me.

No more.

I also know that I have infected bed sores, as when mom is worried she either goes very quiet, or talks incessantly in a slightly unnatural chirpy tone. She started doing just that about three days back, when early in the morning, she had me winched up and out of bed, and was changing the pads that I now wear. I haven't lost my sense of smell, that is for sure. In fact it is a generally well known belief that when we lose one sense, or set of senses, the other ones compensate, becoming stronger and more acute. So, I didn't need anyone to point out that the smell coming from that end of me was not healthy.

What did strike me as odd though was mom not demanding that I consider going into hospital. She usually does. Maybe she had a quiet word with one of the doctors that know me well, as she has most of them on speed dial on her phone. My mom is quite a force to be reckoned with as I have previously mentioned, and I would imagine that some of the doctors in the hospital had to go to quite some lengths to be able to refuse to give her their home numbers too.

Yeah, she is a piece of work all right.

So, I am in a bed in the intensive care unit in a wing of the hospital that I am amazingly not that aux fait with. Surprise, surprise eh? They have me hooked up to a bunch of drips and monitors, but I still feel feverish, then too cold, then too hot again. I have come to know infection quite well over the years. He sits by the bed, reading the magazines and papers left there. He may as well as I can't reach out and pick one up. It always amused me that to this day, people still bring me magazines. I guess it's stuff that you can buy easily in the gift shops, and the big Mark & Spencers concessions that sit in most major hospitals nowadays. I know they mean well, and I know that they know that little Sis will read them out loud to me later in the evenings, when mom and dad have gone home. So not totally thoughtless eh? She knows my taste well, and never reads articles about bands or performers that I have no interest in.

Speaking of little sisters, here she is now. The door to the room whispers open and she steps quietly into the room. Her face tells me that she is fighting with her emotions, and not winning either. I can see that she is very close to tears, and just seeing that brings my own tears, hot and burning on my already quite hot face. She leans in with a hanky and wipes them away. I roll my eyes as if to tell her to get off, but she knows that I value her instincts and always have. When my nose runs, she is the one person who always spots it and quietly gives it a wipe.

She perches gingerly on the corner of the bed, taking care not to sit on a wire, or to disrupt the air flow being piped into my lungs. She looks so sad, that I can feel my heart welling up with feelings. It's almost overwhelming and for a second I struggle to catch my breath. Finally I do though, and the susurration of the machine, and the occasional beep from one of the monitors is all that we can hear. There are no words now. Not for me anyway. If I could have only one wish, it would be to tell her that I love her. But I cannot. I also cannot tell her how proud of her I am, and how she is just about the best person that it has ever been my privilege to know. But she knows all of that. It doesn't have to be spoken out loud. Not between us.

Not now.

29

Goodbye

I guess I was never looking to last until I was 90 years old, and living out my life in some nursing home in Devon, but this still feels too soon. I am only 26 years old after all. I know that must sound insane to some of you reading this, as you may be asking yourself if you would even want to go on, what with all of the challenges that being quadraplegic brings...but I do. I truly do. You might too if the fortunes were reversed.

I have had a good life. All 26 years of them. I never thought that I would be able to say that. But it turns out that it is true. It didn't work out in the way that I had planned. Not in a million freakin' years in fact, but I still love that old saying: *'How do you make God laugh? Tell him your plans.'*

As for the plans that I had for my life...well I never imagined anything like this. I was convinced that the band was going to experience some level of success. We were so close after all. I could almost touch it and taste it on my tongue. But even earlier than that, if you had told me when I left six form at 18 years old that I would be wheelchair bound, and locked inside of a silent prison from the age of 25 years old, I would have laughed in your face. Maybe. But then, when I saw that serious look in your eyes, the laughter would have caught in my throat, and I may have run screaming off the edge of a cliff. However, we don't get to see our futures. God doesn't play things that way. No, when he/she/it plays cards they keep a pretty good poker face, and boy do they nearly always get dealt a good hand?

Time-and-time again.

It turns out that I don't get the average life-expectancy of 80 or so years, or whatever the average age is now. For me, Callum Ross, I got 26 years, and one of those years I got to spend sitting down, talking through a computer programme, to a world that is filled with colour, sound and movement. I learned a lot by sitting still. Things that I would never have imagined way back when I was singing in the band, and hoping to become the next big pop star on the planet. Or, at the very least to create enough of a ripple with the music and the words that I sang.

It turns out that I found another voice. One that is not quite as melodic or pleasing to the ear as my singing voice (if I do say so myself) but nonetheless it still reached around the globe, and moved people in the way that I always hoped that it would. No, my voice became that of the written word, and as I finish off this book, you need to know that it is due to be published in about 20 or so languages around the world. It turns out that you don't have to become a rock star to get a name for yourself after all. Whilst this type of book may not be quite as rock'n'roll as singing on stage at London's O2, or Madison Square Gardens, I have enjoyed knowing that I will still be able to reach an audience in a way that still touches people...and maybe even change a few of their lives. Just that little bit.

I could opine the fact that I may not have slept with quite as many 'fems' as I was hoping but it turns out that with a vivid imagination, born of necessity, anything is possible. Virtually. Besides which quality is better than quantity, and my relationship with Elspeth was definitely quality. Not in any way the kind, or shape of relationship that would suit everyone, but it sure suited me. Well, both of us hopefully!

There are worse things than dying as it turns out. I now believe (and accept) that to be an immutable truth. There is not having lived at all. Or at least not fully because we let our fears, or cautions, or self-doubt or hideous low-self esteems get in the way. And that isn't right. We can, if the circumstances aren't quite right, or the wind is blowing in the wrong direction, hide away from all that life has to offer. I would hate for that to ever be true for me. Even with all my limitations I have never been *small.*

It seems that the biggest imposition that I have now is that I am getting a short life. I have lived and loved as fully as anyone could want in the years that I was given. I have tried my absolute hardest to be the best Callum Ross that I can be. There is, after all, only one of me on the whole planet. A pretty rare and fine distinction if I say so myself.

It turns out too, that I was right about one thing...everything teaches. Everything. There is so much more to life than I ever imagined, and the irony of that statement is that over the last few months imagining is something that I have to do. I imagine myself scaling sheer rock faces, and fighting against giant sea-swells in the atlantic. I imagine myself curled up in front of a huge, roaring fire in some log cabin somewhere, with a woman who makes me happy just to be alive. We are laying in each other's arms with big warming glasses of red wine. We laugh easily, and the simplest pleasures like seeing the flames of the fire reflected in her dark eyes are all I need.

I also realise that life doesn't have a beginning, a middle, or an end. It is constant. We are inside of it all of the time. Kind of like we are all a part of an Inner Life....not just me.

It seems to me now that what we perceive as *real life*, turns out to be mostly illusions, and I for one am happy with that as my final thought. And let it be my final prayer.

And as I drift towards whatever lies beyond this breathing in-and-out life, I find myself wishing that I could go outside, just one last time, and stand there in the darkness of the winter's night. I would love to look up as the snow falls softly around me and watch as the frigid, delicate flakes tumble out of the darkness and into the light. I would love to feel that sharp coldness on my skin. More than that though, I wish that I could look over my shoulder and see my footprints in the fresh snow.

Just one last time.

30

Afterword

I wanted to say thank you for reading this book. It means a lot to me that people spend the time, and some of their hard-earned wages, to jump on-board and take a journey into the unknown with me. And that the places that we go are often as unknown to me as they are to you dear reader is an absolute truth. I get to sit in front of my laptop wondering where in the hell this is all coming from. Constantly! I admit however, that almost every single time it feels like an honour. In fact, I am grateful for just being able to do this. Sure, I don't make any money at it...but oddly that doesn't seem to trouble me too much; at the moment. I will be the first to thrust my hand into the air and beseech the gods of writing and goodwill to allow me to in the future, but for now, the writing is the reward. Taking the journey with the character's, especially as we are on Covid-lockdown has made the days seem just that little more interesting.

Just that little more manageable too.

If you read Stephen King's book, *On Writing*, he says what I and I am sure countless other authors have said - or at the very least thought - that he wonders where the words and the stories come from. I believe that the characters help. At least, if they have enough flesh and substance on their bones, then the stories spill from their mouths, and it was a privilege to sit with Callum as he spoke through me. The irony of that sentence is not lost on me either, and I rather came to like him. Very much in fact. I find that I am crying as I type that. I did mention that Autoimmune Encephalitis has magnified my emotions by about 50%... and I am sticking to that story when it comes to my crying.

Many times I have asked myself (and anybody that cares to listen) if there is any point to writing books if nobody ever reads them. The same applies to music, if I write a song and record it...does it have a life, a validity, if nobody ever listens to it? The only thing I can conclude is, that rather like the old buddhist question, *'If a tree falls in a forest and no one is around to hear it, does it make a sound?'* I guess that there is no clear answer. I will never know. My friends all say that if I enjoy writing, then does it matter how many people read my books? I cannot lie...for me, the answer is YES.

It matters to me.

I have always loved the old Zen koan, *'what is the sound of one hand clapping?'* There is no logical answer to many such buddhist statements, and maybe there shouldn't be too. They entertain us, and make us step sideways, and that's good enough. It seems to me that human beings torture themselves chasing their tails for a lifetime (for an eternity) asking questions like 'why me?' The response to that one is easy though....why not you?

All I know is that whenever someone says that they have read one of my books, or listened to a piece of music that I have made, then somewhere I hear the sound of that tree falling in the woods and it comforts me that it didn't go unnoticed. That it didn't die alone. That would seem to me to be just about the loneliest thing in the world.

Even trees need to be loved eh?

It wasn't until I was 100 pages in that I also realised that the book is about loneliness. As I wrote it I was having my own struggle with the whole Covid/lockdown thing as many people are...or were. Being single and living alone is okay when there is a constant drip set up of phone calls, trips to meet friends, to the beach, to stay over at someone else's house, or simply to head out for a beer of an evening. The unremitting day-in-day-out isolation aspect of lockdown I have found really tough if I am brutally honest. After all, it has been a year now, and like Callum my thoughts have turned to suicide on more occasions than I would care to look at straight on, or to shake a stick at.

That he actually has family around him in his locked-in world, seems (or seemed) immaterial in a way that even as I type I don't fully understand. Maybe I am looking too closely for similarities to my own life, in what is essentially a work of fiction. But don't *they* say that real life is stranger than fiction.

Every single day, for the last however many months has been a pretty good replica of the one that preceded it, and at times I had no idea how I was going to survive it. As I type, we are about three months from the predicted *'end'* when most people will have been vaccinated and we can all return to some semblance of normality. Potentially that is. Quite as to what that will look like I don't have a flamin' clue.

All I know now, is that there were so many aspects of the book and Callum's world that wove into mine. He became a voice for some of the isolation that I have felt throughout my life, some of the fury and hatred too. I can't and won't deny it. That he was (initially) unable to communicate was not lost on me, and the scenes where he is convinced that he is talking out loud is really only a parallel to my own feelings of being virtually invisible for many years. What is not visible to anyone, and this is truly significant in my opinion, are their needs, their thoughts and emotions.

When you see a person on the street who to all intents and purposes looks fine on the outside, do you see their ghosts? Do you see what they crave? And I am not talking about a better car, or a bigger house. No, I am talking about what would make them feel less desperate, less sad, alone, angry, or lost.

Looks are very deceiving, almost impish in their wicked sense of humour and deceptions. And therein lies the huge tragedy in the *invisibility* of mental illness. Oh...and I am not talking solely about diagnosed brain diseases, or inherited disorders, or clinical depression, or chemical imbalances. No, I am talking about depression. A disease that can affect any one of us at any given time; given the right (or wrong) circumstances.

So, if this isn't too odd, I want to thank Callum for giving me a voice, when maybe I really needed it. His character came as a surprise to me. When I started the book I was sure that he would want to die, and that he would find a way. What he did instead was to turn everything on its head and he learned to adapt to a level of adversity that would humble anyone with a heart still beating in their chest. I agree with Callum wholeheartedly (interesting choice of words) when he said, *'what we perceive as real, turns out to be just illusions.'*

The final scene where he is with his sister and they are just sitting together in comfortable silence was very hard for me to write. It took me completely by surprise and it never ceases to amaze me how real-life informs fiction. There were parallels that arose where he is not able to tell her that he loves her, and the loss of my mother who had died of cancer hid until I was typing it. The cancer removed her ability to talk in the last day-or-so of her life and when I finally got to see her the evening before she died, she could only lay a hand on my head.

I never got to hear her say those three precious little words that seem to inspire a billion films, books and song lyrics. That still hurts inside of me, rather like a slow healing wound that flares up from time-to-time. The reaction that writing the scene had was pretty overwhelming as I sat behind (I always think that should be - in front of) my laptop and cried hard. Wept to be totally honest. Just how powerful fiction can be, is certainly not lost on me. It never has been. Books have been a source of joy and deep, deep feeling of connection for me, throughout my life.

I hope that you enjoyed Callum's journey, and like me, feel better for having known him.

No matter how briefly...

Authors Note

Oh, and to those two lost and badly frightened school kids still clinging to each other, deep in the thick of the woods, as the shadows of the early evening grow long.

'Hang in there, help is on it's way.'

Young man, seize every minute
of your time. The days fly by;
ere long you too will grow old.

If you believe me not,
see there, in the courtyard, how the frost
glitters white and cold and cruel
on the grass that once was green.

Do you not see that you and I
are as the branches of one tree?
With your rejoicing,
comes my laughter; with your sadness
start my tears.

Love, could life be otherwise
with you and me?

Tzu-yeh (translated by Bruce Lee)

31

References

The Power of One - Eckhart Tolle

Four Weddings and a Funeral - Director: Mike Newell

Notting Hill - Director: Roger Michell

The Frost - Tzu yeh (translated by Bruce Lee)

Ghosts - David Sylvian, Japan

Streets of Philadelphia - Bruce Springsteen

A course in miracles - Marianne Williamson

I dream of Wires - words/music - Gary Numan

Down in the Park - words/music - Gary Numan

Tao Te Ching - Lao Tzu

Printed in Great Britain
by Amazon